NYMPH ~~Li~~

MUSIC & LYRICS BY
COLE PORTER

BOOK BY
STEVE MACKES
& MICHAEL WHALEY

BASED ON THE NOVEL BY
JAMES LAVER

A SAMUEL FRENCH ACTING EDITION

SAMUEL
FRENCH
FOUNDED 1830

SAMUELFRENCH.COM

IMPORTANT BILLING AND CREDIT
REQUIREMENTS

Nymph Errant
opened at the Chichester Festival Theatre
on August 5 , 1999

Cast

Evangeline Edwards	RAE BAKER
Joyce Arbuthnot-Palmer	HELEN ANKER
Henrietta Bamberg	ALISON CARTER
Bertha	RUBY-MARIE HUTCHINSON
Madeline St. Maure	ISABELLE GEORGES
Miss Pratt	
The Cocotte	MARILYN CUTTS
Mrs. Bamberg	
Aunt Ermyntrude	

and

MARK ADAMS

The Orchestra

Keyboards	JO STEWART
Flute/Violin	HELEN DUFFY
Bass/Percussion	JOFF MORGAN
Director	ROGER REDFARN
Designer	HUGH DURRANT
Musical Arrangements/	
Musical Director	JO STEWART
Choreographer	NIKKI WOOLLASTON
Lighting Designer	NIGEL HOLLOWELL HOWARD
Sound Designer	GREGORY CLARKE *for Aura Sound*
Orchestrations	ADRIAN BULLERS
Music Management	BILL OCCLESHAW
Costume Supervisor	DIANE WILLIAMS
Company Manager	PHILIP DEVERELL
Stage Manager	JO WEEKS
Deputy Stage Manager	ADAM HAVOC
Assistant Stage	
Managers	SUE O'BRIIEN
	CAROLINE BURNETT
Sound Engineer	JASON BARNES
Minerva Carpenter	KARL MEIER

NYMPH ERRANT

In that it has never had a major professional revival, *NYMPH ERRANT* has been until now one of the greatest "lost" musicals of the post-war years; it is also the most important of all Cole Porter's scores never to have enjoyed a Broadway run.

Its history is complex and curious. Early in 1933, the London impresario Charles Cochran (who had already given Gertrude Stein and Noël Coward some of their major stage and musical hits) bought the stage rights in a novel written by a young and then very junior Keeper at the Victoria and Albert Museum, later to make his name as one of the most distinguished of all art and costume curators, James Laver.

Cochran's first idea was to get Laver's novel turned into a play. It was Gertie who convinced him to go for the musical and when Noël declined the commission ("I am not the kind of hired hack who can be summoned by Miss Lawrence to convert others' work into vehicles for her"), Gertie and Cochran turned to his nearest American equivalent, Cole Porter.

Porter loved the novel, and gave it his best shot — the score included three of his greatest hits ("Experiment," "The Physician" and Elizabeth Welch's solo number, the one that introduced her to London stardom, "Solomon"). However, its total and utter Englishness meant that the score never achieved an afterlife on Broadway or film and it is now so unknown in America that the sleeve notes for one recent recording solemnly announce the score to have been based on "Margaret Kennedy's The Constant Nymph," a somewhat different novel.

Gertie was by then living with Douglas Fairbanks Jr. and wrote proudly to her old revue co-star Bea Little that they had "just taken a house in Berkeley Square." "In that case," replied Bea sharply, "you will have to put it back again at once." Gertie had also spent these many years telling the American satirist Alexander Woollcott (*THE MAN WHO CAME TO DINNER*) how well her only daughter was doing at school in Paris. "And what," asked Alexander, tiring of the correspondence at last, "does she teach there?"

Cochran was determined to spare no expense on *NYMPH ERRANT*; Romney Brent was to adapt and direct, Doris Zinekisen to do sets and costumes and for the choreography he brought over, ten years before *OKLAHOMA!*, a young American dancer called Agnes de Mille, whose diary of the show is a little masterpiece in itself. Cole Porter she found a "small, finely boned little man with a round doll head, like a marionette;" as for Gertie, "she is unreliable, chaotic, undisciplined, she can't dance and she can't sing, but who cares? She's a great blazing star even in rehearsal; she delivers; she leads the field; she breaks the tape; her best foot is always forward."

American interest in the show, even at its Manchester try-out, was so great that for the first time in history an entire radio crew was sent over from New York by NBC to broadcast reaction. Gertie on that Manchester opening night did the first-ever live transatlantic broadcast.

Cochran fired one or two lesser members of the cast on tour, including a singer he notably described on stage as "like a Czarina vomiting," and not without troubles they moved south to the Adelphi for much re-rehearsal. The first night, as so often with Gertie and Cochran, was a vast social success but critics next morning were somewhat less impressed. One described Porter's score as "minor-key Coward" and another thought *NYMPH ERRANT* "a pantomime for intellectuals, parched in sentiment and unrelentingly 'witty,' which is the one thing English audiences really hate in musicals."

Nevertheless, Gertie and Elizabeth Welch scored huge personal triumphs and backstage Gertie went on "collecting jewels as other people collect gramophone records;" (Agnes de Mille again) "her energy is legendary on stage and off, and her chic and fun set the style in whatever city or theatre she graces."

NYMPH ERRANT ran on at the Adelphi through the winter of 1933/4, achieving a run of five months and 154 performances. After it closed, there were constant rumors that it would be seen next season on Broadway, but though Gerite did one or two American concert performances of it in later years, the show proved essentially untranslatable in its local references. A decade later, another of her great hits, LADY IN THE DARK, would find it similarly difficult to cross the ocean in the other direction.

Sheridan Morley, 1999

CHARACTERS
(6 female and 1 male)

Evangeline Edwards: English, young and beautiful but unwise to the ways of the world. Her journey is one of growth and learning as she goes from a young schoolgirl to a woman who finally, after much trial and error, finds herself and real love.

Henrietta Bamberg: American and beautiful; speaks with a broad midwest accent; shows irreverent freedom in her speech and manner.

Madeline St. Maure: A French beauty of the sullen type but quite vivacious in temperament. In spite of her "*Jeune Fille*" air, she has a latent voluptuous quality.

Joyce Arbuthnot-Palmer: English country. She is very hearty and always talks through a smile. Would rather spend her time with or on a horse.

Bertha: German; with a zaftig body and the kind of pretty face that heavy girls so often possess.

*Miss Pratt: Tall, prim and proper; very English. In spite of her reserved school teacher looks, there is passion within her, expressed in the advice she gives her students.

*The Cocotte: Once a great courtesan, she is now a little world-weary and tired. Shunned by the younger women and resigned that her time has passed, there is a noble sadness about her.

*Mrs. Bamberg: Henrietta's rich American mother who is spending thousands of dollars for her daughter to marry a title.

*Aunt Ermyntrude: Evangeline's dotty sweet old aunt in Oxford.

**Andre de Croissant: Sophisticated, handsome French impresario; when excited, he is slightly over the top and very dramatic.

**Alexi Gregorgevitch Stukin: Manic-depressive Russian orchestra leader who imagines himself madly in love with Evangeline.

**Fritz: The German nudist who takes Evangeline to a nudist colony in Bavaria.

**Count Ferdinand: The Count who comes to Evangeline's rescue and takes her to Venice.

**Constantine Koumoudouropolos: The Greek shipping magnate who wins Evangeline in a card game.

**Kassim: The big, burly, and blustering Turkish soldier who has an affinity for silk. He sells Evangeline and Bertha into slavery, causing them to become harem girls.

**Ali: The palace Eunuch who is a fan of Evangeline and treats her as an equal.

**Victor Calverston: The young man desperately in love with Evangeline, whom she keeps encountering throughout her adventures.

*All played by the same actress   ***All played by the same actor*

SCENE BREAKDOWN

ACT 1

Scene 1   Belle Vue Pension / Lausanne Rail Station

Scene 2   A Train Compartment

Scene 3   The Square at Neauville Sur Mer

Scene 4   The Gala at Neauville Sur Mer

Scene 5   Alexi's Apartment and a Cafe in Paris

Scene 6   Pierre Fort's Apartment Paris

Scene 7   The Grand Hotel Kurzdorfer

Scene 8   A Grand Palazzo in Venice

ACT II

Scene 1   Ruins in Smyrna / A Tavern

Scene 2   Desert / Harem Quarters

Scene 3   Gare de Lyon, Paris / Opening Night Folie de Paris / Jewelry Shop

Scene 4   A Garden in Oxford

SONGS

ACT I

THEY ALL FALL IN LOVE	Evangeline, Joyce, Henrietta, Madeline & Bertha
EXPERIMENT	Pratt, Evangeline, Joyce, Henrietta, Madeline & Bertha
BAD FOR ME	Evangeline & Andre
THE COCOTTE	The Cocotte
HOW COULD WE BE WRONG	Alexi & Evangeline
YOU'D BE SO NICE TO COME HOME TO	Victor
THE GREAT INDOORS	Joyce
BACK TO NATURE	Fritz & Evangeline
YOU'RE TOO FAR AWAY	Victor
THEY'RE ALWAYS ENTERTAINING	Mrs. Bamberg, Henrietta & Servants
GEORGIA SAND	Henrietta
NYMPH ERRANT	Evangeline, Constantine, Joyce, Henrietta, Madeline & Bertha

ACT II

RUINS	Evangeline & Company
BACK TO NATURE / Reprise	Cross Over Music (Orchestration)
BAD FOR ME/Reprise	Harem Intro Music (Orchestration)
THE PHYSICIAN	Evangeline
CAZANOVA	The Tango (Orchestration)
SOLOMON	Bertha
WHEN LOVE COMES YOUR WAY	Victor
SI VOUS AIMEZ LES POITRINES	Madeline & Company
AT LONG LAST LOVE	Evangeline
EXPERIMENT / Finale	Evangeline, Victor, Miss Pratt, Joyce, Madeline, Henrietta & Bertha

OVERTURE

ACT I

Scene 1

Scene: Pension Belle Vue / Rail Station, Lausanne.
Time: A May evening, 1933.
*At Rise: The house curtain goes up, revealing an act curtain featuring
          a patchwork of hotel luggage labels from European grand
          hotels of the period.*

*(At end of overture, spot hits MISS PRATT, a lady of a certain age.
She steps forward with an arm full of roses and walks down center as she addresses the audience.)*

PRATT. Yes well. What a great gathering of alumni we have
here. I recognize so many former students. *(Taking her glasses and
peering into the first row.)* And it is evident in your faces, a bit older
and longer perhaps, that the lessons of time and gravity, taught at this
school for so long, are working still—yes, in some cases working
overtime—continuing to teach each and every one of you. Nevertheless, it warms my heart to see you here in Switzerland at the Pension
Belle-Vue. And now if you will excuse me I must wish a few very
special girls bon voyage.

(EVANGELINE comes running in.)

EVANGELINE. Miss Pratt.
PRATT. Evangeline Edwards I shall miss your sweet smile in my
classroom. *(Hands her a rose.)* This is for you. *(EVANGELINE takes
the rose, tries to speak, PRATT continues on.)* No, no, not a word.
You will make me misty. You're heading for the station?
(EVANGELINE nods.) Tell the other girls I will join them there
shortly.

(PRATT exits, lights down to spot on EVANGELINE.)

EVANGELINE. The other girls:

*(Pool of light comes up on JOYCE in a pose of the period; she is
dressed to kill for travel.)*

Joyce Arbuthnot-Palmer, a fellow English chum.

(Another pool comes up on HENRIETTA posed and dressed for travel.)
Sassy Henrietta Bamberg, our only American.

(Another pool comes up on BERTHA posed and dressed for travel.)
That would be big-hearted Bertha.

(Another pool comes up on MADELINE posed and dressed for travel.)
Naughty, saucy Madeline St. Maure, French of course.

(Lights out on girls.) Oh but look at the time, I really must fly. Taxi!

(EVANGELINE runs off as lights are up on JOYCE and HENRIETTA.)

JOYCE. Bertha, please we're going to be late.
HENRIETTA. Yeah, get a move on. Some of us have trains to catch.

(BERTHA enters loaded down with suitcases.)

BERTHA. Why must I always carry the suitcases?
HENRIETTA. Because, my dear Bertha, as I've said to Joyce so often, you have the constitution of an ox, not to mention the back of a pack mule.

(BERTHA exits.)

JOYCE. It's hard to believe that four years have passed and we are finally graduated.
HENRIETTA. Yes and what a waste of four years it was.
JOYCE. Henrietta how can you say that? We learned a little of everything.
HENRIETTA. And a lot of nothing.

(BERTHA enters, pushing a luggage cart; MADELINE sits on top of the bags.)

MADELINE. Ah, mon petite amies, c'est magnifique, un reunion des filles!
BERTHA. Madeline, you are not ze queen. Get off ze cart!
HENRIETTA. Yes, you're making the other baggage look cheap.
MADELINE. I think you mean *chic.*
BERTHA. She means cheap.

JOYCE. But where is Evangeline?

MADELINE. Where is Evangeline? I will close my eyes and think.

HENRIETTA. Just pull your skirt down. It might be rude if people were to see your thinking cap.

MADELINE. Americans can be so annoying. Or perhaps it is just *this* American.

BERTHA. After today, you could never see her again.

MADELINE. Yes, isn't that wonderful?

BERTHA. No, nein. It is sad. I think I will miss everyone here.

JOYCE. I think I see Evangeline now. Bertie, go tell her to hurry. Bitte?

(BERTHA nods and exits.)

HENRIETTA. You have done such a splendid job of training her. What's your secret, treats?

JOYCE. Do you have to be so cruel?

HENRIETTA. Yes, I think I do.

(EVANGELINE enters carrying the rose, followed by BERTHA with bags.)

EVANGELINE. Thanks awfully darling, you're a lamb. Put them there. *(To the others.)* Here we are one last time. Before going our separate ways. Me, back to Oxford.

BERTHA. I'm to University in Berlin.

HENRIETTA. It's Venice for me. A long, long summer with Mama.

JOYCE. I'm for Brussels, then on to London.

MADELINE. And I am bound for who knows where?

HENRIETTA. Isn't that right next to no place in particular?

EVANGELINE. It doesn't matter where we're heading. With our schooling complete, now it's time for each of us to embark on a new mission, a quest.

MUSIC: EXPERIMENT (STING)

BERTHA. A quest for what?

EVANGELINE. Why, to find true love.

JOYCE. Love? What an idea. Do you think it will ever happen to me?

MADELINE. You mean it hasn't already?

JOYCE. Uh, well, uh ....

HENRIETTA. Love happens to everyone. Sooner or later. Like

it or not.

JOYCE. Really?

EVANGELINE. Yes, really. Henrietta's right. I assure you, one day we will all be madly in love with someone ... or two ... or three.

MUSIC: THEY ALL FALL IN LOVE

EVANGELINE.
EACH YEAR, WHEN SPRING, QUITE UNINVITED,
GIVES A GARDEN PARTY TO THE WORLD UNITED,
EV'RYONE GETS SO EXCITED
THEY DON'T KNOW WHAT THEY'RE THINKING OF.
FOLKS WHO'VE SPENT THE WINTER FREEZIN',
WHIFF THE BALMY BREEZE AND SIMPLY LOSE THEIR REASON.
THEY KNOW IT'S THE OPEN SEASON,
FOR FALLING IN LOVE.

THE YOUNG FALL, THE OLD FALL,
THE RED-HOT MAMMAS, AND THE COLD FALL,
FROM THE LILY WHITE TO THE BLACK AS NIGHT,
THEY ALL FALL IN LOVE.

HENRIETTA.
THE FOOLS FALL, THE WISE FALL,
THE WETS, THE SPRINKLED, AND THE DRYS FALL,
FROM THE MEN WHO DRINK TO THE MEN WHO WINK
THEY ALL FALL IN LOVE.

~~JOYCE.~~ MADELINE
YOU MAY BELIEVE YOUR BROKER IS VERY MEDIOCRE
AT PLAYING WITH YOUR STOCKS AND BONDS.
AT BUSINESS HE MAY BLUNDER
BERTHA.
YET HE'S A PERFECT WONDER WHEN HE PLAYS WITH
    BLONDES.

HENRIETTA.
OLD MAIDS WHO OBJECT FALL,
OLD MEN YOU WOULD NEVER SUSPECT FALL.
JOYCE.
EVEN BABIES, WHO CAN HARDLY CRAWL, FALL?
HENRIETTA.
'CAUSE THEY ALL FALL IN LOVE.

MADELINE.
THE WAGS FALL, THE BOOBS FALL,
THE GOLD-BRICK SELLERS AND THE RUBES FALL,
  JOYCE.
FROM THE UNDERBRED TO THE OVERFED?
  ALL.
THEY ALL FALL IN LOVE.

  EVANGELINE.
THE GOOD VERY OFT FALL,
  MADELINE.
THE HARD-SHELLED BAPTISTS AND THE SOFT FALL,
  HENRIETTA.
JUST TO PROVE THEY BELIEVE, IN THE FALL OF EVE,
  ALL.
THEY ALL FALL IN LOVE.

  HENRIETTA.
THE SOLEMN UNDERTAKER IS SHYER THAN A QUAKER,
AS LONG AS HE IS FILLING GRAVES,
BUT LET HIM MEET A MISSUS
WHO HASN'T PREJUDICES, AND HE MISBEHAVES.
  BERTHA.
THE ANGELS ON HIGH FALL,
  HENRIETTA.
AND MEN LIKE LINDBERGH WHO CAN FLY FALL,
  EVANGELINE.
EVEN BOXERS MUCH TOO PURE TO FALL, FALL,
  ALL.
'CAUSE THEY ALL FALL IN LOVE.

(At the song's end, a young man, VICTOR CALVERSTON crosses the platform, absent-mindedly looking about; he bumps into EVAN-GELINE; she drops her flower, which he steps on. The two make eye contact. VICTOR, by his expression, is immediately smitten.)

VICTOR. Excuse me, I am so clumsy.
EVANGELINE. You're standing on my flower.

(He picks up the now bent and battered rose and offers it to her.)

VICTOR. And to think, I am a horticulturist.

EVANGELINE. You did wonders for this. It's ruined.

(She lets the flower fall to the ground.)

VICTOR. I'm Victor Calverston. And I really do apologize. I wish you would allow me to—

JOYCE. Vangy, stop talking to strangers and come over here.

(EVANGELINE turns and joins her friends; VICTOR looks longingly after her; he picks up the fallen rose, regarding it like a jewel. As he exits, EVANGELINE removes four little packages from her purse and distributes them.)

EVANGELINE. Here we are chums. One for each of you.

HENRIETTA. What's this?

JOYCE. *(Ripping the paper off.)* Oh, Vangy, you silly girl.

EVANGELINE. It's nothing. They're all the same. I just couldn't resist.

BERTHA. *(Opening hers.)* A little pin.

JOYCE. Of a knight?

HENRIETTA. In shining armor. How fabulous.

BERTHA. *(Pinning hers on.)* I will wear it always. Close to my heart.

EVANGELINE. I have one myself. see? *(Lifting her collar flap to reveal the pin.)* I like to imagine, under the armor, maybe it's a woman in there. Embarking on an adventure. A female knight errant.

JOYCE. Or a nymph errant.

HENRIETTA. On a quest like us, to find true love and adventure. Why not?

MADELINE. Why not? Because, ~~mon~~ cherie, that is not the way of the world. Women do not travel the countryside having adventures. And Evangeline, you will never find that prince charming. Why, you will probably end up an old maid living with your aunt.

HENRIETTA. Oh Pooh!

(Except for MADELINE, the girls busily put on their pins.)

JOYCE. But I do say, I rather like this nymph errant idea. I'm sure she would ride atop a magnificent steed. Its head back, nostrils flared, muscles bulging, flanks heaving—

MADELINE. I would like this steed's address.

EVANGELINE. Are we talking about horses or men?

HENRIETTA. What's the difference? They're both overbearing beasts.

EVANGELINE. You ask what's the difference? You're missing the most important thing of all.

MADELINE. The size of the man's bank account?

HENRIETTA. I think Evie means love and romance.

EVANGELINE. Yes. I'm talking about a deep, deep, singular commitment to another person.

JOYCE. Like the way you felt about the doctor?

BERTHA. Last year when you got the flu.

HENRIETTA. You were sick in love with him.

EVANGELINE. *(Blushing.)* Oh! Why— And I was just beginning to forget him!

(The other girls laugh as MISS PRATT enters, carrying four roses.)

MISS PRATT. I want to remember you all just like this. Young, beautiful and happy.

HENRIETTA. *(Brightening and being the hostess.)* Look girls, the chemistry department has arrived.

JOYCE. Miss Pratt, thank you for coming to bid us farewell.

PRATT. You girls have been my favorite students. And I couldn't let you leave these. A flower for each of you. To serve as a symbol of your future growth. Evangeline already got hers. *(Distributing the flowers.)* As you go out into the world, like the rose, you too will open your pedals.

HENRIETTA. *(Looking at Madeline.)* Well, if she opened her pedals any wider—

MADELINE. At least mine aren't beginning to droop.

PRATT. Girls, girls, soon, like carbon-dioxide or some other gaseous substance, you will dissipate into all parts of the continent.

HENRIETTA. Any last instructions for us before we go?

PRATT. Instructions, about what?

BERTHA. Life.

JOYCE. Love.

MADELINE. Men!

PRATT. Well, I do have one suggestion.

MUSIC: EXPERIMENT

PRATT.
BEFORE YOU LEAVE THESE PORTALS
TO MEET LESS FORTUNATE MORTALS,
THERE'S JUST ONE PARTING MESSAGE I WOULD GIVE TO
    YOU
YOU HAVE ALL LEARNED RELIANCE
ON THE SACRED TEACHINGS OF SCIENCE
SO I HOPE, THROUGH LIFE, YOU NEVER WILL DECLINE,
IN SPITE OF PHILISTINE
DEFIANCE

TO DO WHAT ALL GOOD SCIENTISTS DO.
EXPERIMENT, MAKE IT YOUR MOTTO DAY AND NIGHT.
EXPERIMENT, AND IT WILL LEAD YOU TO THE LIGHT.
THE APPLE ON THE TOP OF THE TREE IS NEVER TOO HIGH
    TO ACHIEVE.

    GIRLS.
JUST TAKE AN EXAMPLE FROM EVE,

    PRATT.
EXPERIMENT
BE CURIOUS, THOUGH INTERFERING FRIENDS MAY FROWN
GET FURIOUS AT EACH ATTEMPT TO HOLD YOU DOWN,
IF THIS ADVICE YOU ONLY EMPLOY,
THE FUTURE CAN OFFER YOU INFINITE JOY.

    GIRLS.
AND MERRIMENT,
EXPERIMENT
AND YOU'LL SEE.

(Goes into a production number (could be tap) that uses luggage carts and suitcases and covers the entire platform.)

    GIRLS.
EXPERIMENT, MAKE IT YOUR MOTTO DAY AND NIGHT.
EXPERIMENT, AND IT WILL LEAD YOU TO THE LIGHT.
THE APPLE ON THE TOP OF THE TREE IS NEVER TOO HIGH
    TO ACHIEVE.
JUST TAKE AN EXAMPLE FROM EVE,

    PRATT & GIRLS.
EXPERIMENT
BE CURIOUS, THOUGH INTERFERING FRIENDS MAY FROWN
GET FURIOUS AT EACH ATTEMPT TO HOLD YOU DOWN,
IF THIS ADVICE YOU ONLY EMPLOY,
THE FUTURE CAN OFFER YOU INFINITE JOY
AND MERRIMENT,
EXPERIMENT
AND YOU'LL SEE.

(At the end of the song, the girls are standing on rear platforms. On applause, they open their respective doors and exit into the train cars leaving MISS PRATT alone SC for blackout.)

End of Scene 1

Scene 2

Scene: Interior of train car.
Time: Immediately following.
At Rise: Center section of train car flies out to reveal interior of railway carriage; seated is ANDRE DE CROISSANT, an attractive Frenchman in his 40's, looking admiringly at the rear view of EVANGELINE hanging out the window.

EVANGELINE. Miss Pratt, my bag, if you please.
PRATT. *(Off stage.)* Good-bye, dear. And don't forget: experiment!
EVANGELINE. *(Pulling bag inside.)* I won't, good-bye!

(There is the sound of a train pulling out. Standing on the seat, EVANGELINE places her bag on the overhead rack. ANDRE watches closely. As she steps down, he feigns reading his book. She settles down to a book of her own. ANDRE glances repeatedly at her; he lights a cigarette.)

ANDRE. *(Indicating the smoke.)* Pardon, Mademoiselle. *(She resumes reading; ANDRE returns to his book, but just for a moment.)* You are English, no?
EVANGELINE. I am English yes.
ANDRE. I love the English.
EVANGELINE. Of course you do.
ANDRE. The English woman she has, how you say, the stately body. She holds her beauty. *(Suddenly, EVANGELINE's eyes widen. She opens her purse and looks inside. She searches her pockets and then the floor, growing increasingly frantic.)* The Spanish, they fade quickly and the Italians, such temperament. As for the Germans—
EVANGELINE. *(Interrupting him.)* I've lost my ticket! What an idiot! I must have left it— Oh, what am I to do?

(ANDRE removes two tickets from a pocket and holds one out.)

ANDRE. Perhaps I may be of assistance, Mademoiselle?
EVANGELINE. This is just dreadful. How am I going to— Where can I— *(Seeing the ticket in his hand.)* What's that?
ANDRE. For you.
EVANGELINE. You always carry an extra, in case you meet a damsel in distress?
ANDRE. Ah, non. You see, my friend she miss the train, and now I have two. One for me and now one for you. It is fortunate, no?

EVANGELINE. Uh … uh … I really can't thank you enough.

ANDRE. *(Under his breath.)* We shall see.

EVANGELINE. Pardon?

ANDRE. Please. It is nothing. You have been at school, yes?

EVANGELINE. This was my last year. I'm completely finished.

ANDRE. Ah non, Mademoiselle, you are only just beginning! The London season starts.

EVANGELINE. I don't live in London. I live in Oxford with my aunt.

ANDRE. With your aunt! What a pity. If I were a young, beautiful woman like you, I would go on the stage.

EVANGELINE. Now, that is something I have never considered.

ANDRE. And why is that?

EVANGELINE. I don't think I have any talent.

ANDRE. Then you are one of the lucky ones. I often find talent only gets in the way. Can you sing?

EVANGELINE. No

ANDRE. Can you dance?

EVANGELINE. Not very well.

ANDRE. Acting?

EVANGELINE. None.

ANDRE. Brava! Where have you been hiding? I can make you the great star. Ah yes, you wear the beautiful clothes. You sit in the beautiful dressing room surrounded by the beautiful baskets of flowers and the young men, very correct, come in and kiss your hand and your arm and your— *(Demonstrating, then stopping himself.)*

EVANGELINE. But it can't be as easy as all that.

ANDRE. No? I own the *Folie de Paris* and there it is moi, Andre de Croissant, who makes the stars. And I would be so very happy to make you.

EVANGELINE. *(Wavering.)* Do you really think I could be a star?

MUSIC: EXPERIMENT (STING)

ANDRE. I implore you. Grab life with the gusto. You must give it a try.

MUSIC: IT'S BAD FOR ME

EVANGELINE.
YOUR WORDS GO THROUGH AND THROUGH ME
AND LEAVE ME TOTALLY DAZED.
FOR THEY DO SUCH STRANGE THINGS TO ME

THEY NEARLY MAKE ME GLOOMY,
FOR YOU, SIR, ARE SO CLEVER, SO OBVIOUSLY "THE TOP,"
I WISH YOU'D GO ON FOREVER, I WISH EVEN MORE YOU'D
    STOP.
OH, IT'S BAD FOR ME, IT'S BAD FOR ME,
THIS KNOWLEDGE THAT YOU'RE GOING MAD FOR ME,
I FEEL CERTAIN MY FRIENDS WOULD BE GLAD FOR ME,
STILL IT'S BAD FOR ME.
IT'S SO GOOD FOR ME, SO NEW FOR ME
TO SEE SOMEONE IN SUCH A STEW FOR ME,
AND WHEN YOU SAY YOU'D DO ALL YOU COULD FOR ME
IT'S SO GOOD FOR ME, IT'S BAD FOR ME,
I FELT TILL YOU WHISPERED TO ME, COMPLETELY LEFT
    ON THE SHELF,
BUT SINCE YOU STARTED TO WOO ME, I'M JUST CRAZY
    ABOUT MYSELF.
IT'S A BOON FOR ME, A BREAK FOR ME
TO HEAR THAT YOUR HEART'S ON THE MAKE FOR ME.
YET NO MATTER HOWEVER APPEALING, I STILL HAVE A
    FEELING
IT'S BAD FOR ME.

*(The tempo picks up as EVANGELINE is chased by ANDRE around
    the train compartment interior.)*

EVANGELINE.
OH, IT'S BAD FOR ME, IT'S BAD FOR ME
THIS KNOWLEDGE THAT YOU'RE GOING MAD FOR ME.
    ANDRE.
I FEEL CERTAIN MY FRIENDS WOULD BE GLAD FOR ME,
    EVANGELINE.
BUT IT'S BAD FOR ME.
IT'S SO GOOD FOR ME, SO NEW FOR ME
TO SEE SOMEONE IN SUCH A STEW FOR ME
AND WHEN YOU SAY YOU'D DO ALL YOU COULD FOR ME
IT'S SO GOOD FOR ME, IT'S BAD FOR ME.

ANDRE. *(All over her.)* Come with me to Neauville Sur Mer and
then on to Paris. By this fall, I promise you will already have a reputa-
tion.
EVANGELINE. *(Breaking away.)* That's rather what I'm afraid
of.
ANDRE. You must trust me. The world needs you. I need you.
Please Miss ... Miss ....
EVANGELINE. Evangeline Edwards.

ANDRE. *(Total recovery.)* Evangeline Edwards! Don't worry we can change that. Ah, I will teach you things in Neauville.

EVANGELINE. Even if I could go, isn't Neauville expensive?

ANDRE. To a beautiful woman, nothing is expensive.

EVANGELINE. I don't know. I'm just not sure. Maybe if we cared for each other. If we had a past, well no, not exactly a past. What I mean— Oh, I wish I knew what I meant!

(Lights up on an image of MADELINE through a scrim.)

MADELINE. Evangeline you will never find that Prince Charming. You will probably end up an old maid living with your aunt.

(Lights out on MADELINE.)

EVANGELINE. Oh really, just watch me!

ANDRE. I would love to watch you. Evangeline, you are young, beautiful and charming! Do not let life pass you by. Say 'yes' to my offer.

EVANGELINE. I must say, I find myself leaning that way.

ANDRE. Lean a little further mon cher.

EVANGELINE. But for a place like Neauville Sur Mer, I have nothing to wear. *(ANDRE lowers a travel case and opens it; he pulls out gowns, each more beautiful than the last; lights down to a pin spot on EVANGELINE.)* Oh ....

MUSIC: BAD FOR ME / REPRISE

(Starts slow and builds in tempo until the end is a full out belt number.)

EVANGELINE.
IT'S SO GOOD FOR ME, SO NEW FOR ME
TO SEE SOMEONE IN SUCH A STEW FOR ME,
AND WHEN YOU SAY YOU'D DO ALL YOU COULD FOR ME
IT'S SO GOOD FOR ME, IT'S BAD FOR ME,
I FELT, TILL YOU WHISPERED TO ME, COMPLETELY LEFT
    ON THE SHELF,
BUT SINCE YOU STARTED TO WOO ME, I'M JUST CRAZY
    ABOUT MYSELF.
IT'S A BOON FOR ME, A BREAK FOR ME,
TO HEAR THAT YOUR HEART'S ON THE MAKE FOR ME,
YET NO MATTER HOWEVER APPEALING, I STILL HAVE A
    FEELING
IT'S BAD FOR ME.

(At the song's end the train car breaks away and splits to wings taking EVANGELINE off, and giving way to an outdoor cafe in Neauville Sur Mer.)

End of Scene 2

Scene 3

Scene: An outdoor cafe in Neauville Sur Mer.   ~~SFX Accordion Music?~~

Time: Several days later.

At Rise: *Lights up on the front of a small cafe on the grand promenade of this seaside resort. Seated at a cafe table is a woman with a long cigarette holder. She wears a large hat and is posed like a poster of the period. Two women stroll nearby, their faces hidden by parasols.*

(ALEXI, a disheveled and quite mad Russian, enters and takes a seat at the table next to the woman.)

WOMAN. Ah Alexi, my young Russian friend, why so sad?

ALEXI. Mad? I'm not mad. Why does everyone think I'm mad?

WOMAN. I said 'sad.' But now that you mention it ....

ALEXI. Oh. It is true I am suffering.

WOMAN. From what? Is it your music? No, I think it must be an affair l'amour.

ALEXI. I cannot speak of it. Nothing, not terror, torture, prison, or all the armies of the world can make me reveal what I am feeling. *(A beat.)* All right. I'm in love.

WOMAN. As I suspected. And who is the object of your anguish?

ALEXI. A beautiful English girl. The young friend of Monsieur de Croissant. Every night they come to the casino and dance before my bandstand. I am so taken with her I want to kill myself.

WOMAN. Dramatic, but not very practical. Why don't you let me help. I shall introduce myself to the young lady and tell her all about you. Well, not all. I will discreetly leave out the fact that you have no money. *(Looking off in the distance.)* I think that is she approaching now.

ALEXI. Look at me. Shaking. I can't face her.

(ALEXI ducks beneath his table as MADELINE enters; the older

woman approaches her.)

WOMAN. Excuse me, I beg your pardon, but my friend here—
(Gesturing in the direction of ALEXI; he is gone.) Where did he go?
Ah, my friend has been admiring you on the casino dance floor.
MADELINE. I have not been at the casino. You are confusing
me with someone else.

*(The older woman returns to her table as EVANGELINE enters.
Looking sophisticated in the latest clothes and hairstyle, she
turns to the wing.)*

EVANGELINE. Yes darling, Madam Arthur's shop. I must have
left them at the counter. I'll be in the cafe. *(Seeing MADELINE and
then to audience.)* You can imagine my surprise when I looked and
there, big as life, was Madeline.
MADELINE. *(Seeing EVANGELINE.)* Evangeline? Mon Dieu I
can't believe my eyes. What are you doing here? And what have you
done to yourself?
EVANGELINE. When in Rome, or in this case, Neauville Sur
Mer. Are you with your parents?
MADELINE. Praise the heavens no.
EVANGELINE. Not a man?
MADELINE. If you must know, I came here with the Comte de
Bigorre, the famous aviator. But we had a fight and poof, he flew
away. You are here with your Aunt?
EVANGELINE. Not exactly.
ANDRE. *(Entering with a pair of sunglasses.)* I found them. I
found them.

*(He presents the glasses to EVANGELINE; MADELINE looks him
over.)*

MADELINE. Not exactly, I should say.
EVANGELINE. Monsieur Andre de Croissant, Madeline St.
Maure. We attended school together.
ANDRE. *(Taking her hand and kissing it.)* Charme, Mademoi-
selle.
MADELINE. Enchante, Monsieur. The two of you are here for
the season?
ANDRE. Oui. Then we return to Paris, where Evangeline will be
my new star.
EVANGELINE. Oh, Andre, I keep telling you, that is just too
ridiculous.
MADELINE. Cheri, you do not want to be a star? Silly girl. If I

had such a chance— *(Giving ANDRE a sexy stare.)* I would jump on it.

ANDRE. *(Aroused.)* Really?

MADELINE. *(Giving him a great view of her cleavage.)* Mais certainement.

ANDRE. *(Wiping his brow with a handkerchief.)* I must make some calls to Paris. My backers. *(To Madeline.)* Would you join us at this evening's gala if you have no other plans?

MADELINE. How very sweet. I would be most charmed. Especially now that I am alone.

ANDRE. Beautiful young women do not remain alone for long. Evangeline, while I attend to business, you and Madeline can go shopping. For this evening's costumes.

(He takes out a wad of money, hands some to EVANGELINE, kisses her hand and exits; the older woman moves closer to EVANGELINE.)

MADELINE. Darling, how very clever of you to find a lovely rich man.

WOMAN. Excuse me, Miss?

EVANGELINE. Have we met?

WOMAN. No. But I was hoping I could speak to you concerning a—

MADELINE. That is impossible. We are in a hurry. And you are intruding. *(To EVANGELINE as she pulls her away.)* We don't want to be seen with a woman like her. She's a Cocotte!

EVANGELINE. A what?

MADELINE. A Cocotte. A courtesan. Once, quite famous. But now what you call a been-has.

WOMAN. *(Watching the girls exit.)* So the young women do not wish to speak with a lady such as myself. Don't worry my dears, your day, will come soon enough.

MUSIC: THE COCOTTE

WOMAN.
WHILE THE LUCKY ONES SIT TOGETHER
WITH NOTHING TO CURSE BUT WEATHER
PERMIT ME TO TELL YOU OF MY SAD FATE.
FOR DUE TO MY GREAT DISCRETION

IN PRACTICING MY PROFESSION
I SUDDENLY WAKE UP TO FIND I DATE.
WHEN LADIES STILL HAD PROPRIETY,

WOMEN LIKE ME WERE COVERED WITH GLORY,
BUT NOW, SINCE THESE DAMNED SOCIETY- WOMEN
INVADED MY TERRITORY

A BUSTED, DISGUSTED COCOTTE AM I,
JUST A FLOP FROM THE TOP TO THE BOTTOM AM I
WHILE THOSE FAT FEMMES DU MONDE
WITH THE MEN WHOM ONCE I OWNED
SPLASH AROUND LIKE HELL-BOUND HIPPOPOTAMI.
SINCE ONLY DAMES WITH THEIR NAMES ON THEIR
        CHEQUES APPEAL
TO MODERN MEN, INSTEAD OF SEX, I NOW HAVE EX-APPEAL.
WHAT WILL MA SAY TO ME
WHEN SHE SEES I'VE TURNED OUT TO BE
AN ANNOYED, UNEMPLOYED COCOTTE?

*INSERT P.27
Dialogue*

AND ON MY TOMBSTONE I TRUST
WILL BE WRITTEN "EXCUSE THE DUST
OF A FAST BUT OUTCLASSED COCOTTE."

(On the last lines, the lights dim to a pin spot on her face. As she exits, the set begins to change to a fantasy garden.)

End of Scene 3

Scene 4

Scene: *The same outdoor square.*
Time: *That same evening.*
At Rise: *"It's Bad for Me" music underscoring comes up in a waltz tempo as the cafe transforms, with lights and trees, into an outdoor pavilion and the setting for the gala.*

(A masked couple in spectacular costumes waltzes across and off. As they cross, a masked girl dressed as Marie Antoinette enters, dancing. She is followed by EVANGELINE, dressed as a Pirouette, ANDRE in a knight's suit of armor complete with visored helmet, and MADELINE in a Cleopatra outfit that barely covers her.)

EVANGELINE. Andre how are you managing?

(ANDRE gestures and mumbles indistinctly.)

MADELINE. The helmet is stuck, no?

EVANGELINE. He said it fit fine at the costume shop. If only we could loosen this visor.

(She tugs at the helmet to ANDRE's discomfort and incoherent protest.)

MADELINE. I have it. We get one of those corkscrews for the wine and pry it loose.

(ANDRE responds with mumbles that express fear for this idea.)

MADELINE. Come with me. I know what to do.

(MADELINE leads ANDRE upstage and off. The COCOTTE enters in costume.)

WOMAN. Oh, Miss, excuse me?

EVANGELINE. You were at the café earlier. You wanted to speak with me?

WOMAN. I am merely the messenger for one who is desperately in love with you.

EVANGELINE. Desperately in love. With me?

WOMAN. It is young Alexi. He conducts the orchestra in the casino.

EVANGELINE. How very odd—

WOMAN. Yes, he can be. Oh, you mean the situation.

EVANGELINE. But also very sweet and charming. Tell the young man that I am greatly flattered, but I am here with a friend. But please, let him know in a nice way, won't you?

WOMAN. Of course. You may count on it. You are very kind.

EVANGELINE. *(Watching the COCOTTE exit; to audience.)* Someone desperately in love with me! It's a lovely thought, but I do have an escort somewhere around here. *(She crosses UR and stops. From behind a column, a laughing MADELINE leans out. Suddenly an arm in familiar knight's armor grabs MADELINE and pulls her back into the dark. EVANGELINE moves away and breaks into tears; ALEXI enters and crosses to her.)* Andre, how could you? And with Madeline of all— *(Seeing ALEXI.)* Ah! How long have you been there?

ALEXI. A moment only. Permit me. I am Alexi Gregorgevitch Stukin.

EVANGELINE. I know who you are. The conductor.

ALEXI. It has been my dream to make your acquaintance.

EVANGELINE. About that, did the woman, your friend, older, tell you—

ALEXI. Her expression alone told me my aspirations were hopeless.

EVANGELINE. And yet, you are still here.

ALEXI. I find hopelessness so irresistibly beautiful. Like you.

EVANGELINE. Listen, Alexi, Georgei—whatever, don't you have an orchestra to—

ALEXI. No more. I quit. How I hate this place. The shoddy pretense. The red lips, painted faces, the fine clothes bought with what? Their own bodies. *(Seeing that she is reacting to this personally.)* Forgive me. You are not like them. You are the reason I stayed.

EVANGELINE. What do you mean?

ALEXI. The first night you came here was the night I had intended to leave. But when I saw you, I became entranced. I knew the Frenchman would never, could never understand your soul. And I hoped— But now, I *must* kill myself *(Beat.)* or perhaps I go to Paris.

EVANGELINE. Please, Alexi. Choose Paris.

ALEXI. I will. If you choose Alexi. If you come with me.

EVANGELINE. Oh. No, I am so unhappy, I'm afraid you would not find me very good company.

ALEXI. You are unhappy? Then let us die together!

EVANGELINE. I'm not quite that unhappy!

MADELINE. *(Off stage.)* Would I have my very own plumes and jewels? Andre, you sweet, lovely man, of course I will be your star. Viva la poitrine!

ALEXI. *(To EVANGELINE.)* There is nothing now to hold you here. Come with me to Paris.

EVANGELINE. *(To audience.)* What should I do? I feel such a fool. *(Looking at her costume.)* I'm even dressed for the part.

ALEXI. You just had a patch of bad luck.

EVANGELINE. Alexi, you're very sweet. You would take things slow? You wouldn't rush me? *(ALEXI nods yes and no appropriately.)* All right, then on to Paris. There's just one problem. I have nothing to wear.

ALEXI. I have some money and prospects. Whatever you want, it is yours.

MUSIC: HOW COULD WE BE WRONG?

ALEXI.
THE MOMENT I SAW YOU AND YOU LOOKED MY WAY,
THAT MOMENT OF MOMENTS I STARTED TO SAY:
"COULD THIS BE MY LONG-LOST DREAM COME TRUE?"
THE MOMENT WE TOUCHED, I KNEW.

EVANGELINE.
HOW COULD WE BE WRONG?
WHEN WE BOTH ARE SO SET ON IT,
HOW COULD WE BE WRONG?
    ALEXI.
OUR LOVE IS SO STRONG
I'D BE WILLING TO BET ON IT,
HOW COULD WE BE WRONG?

    BOTH.
WHY SHOULD IT EVER DIE?
DARLING, YOU AND I
ARE TOO WONDERFULLY HAPPY TODAY
TO THROW IT AWAY.
NOW, LIFE IS A SONG
IF WE BUILD A DUET ON IT,
HOW COULD WE BE WRONG?

(A 1930's type map flies in that traces their route from Neauville to Paris. They move behind a scrim, in what is suggestive of a moving rail car. Singing, they change clothes as the set changes.)

    BOTH.
WHY, SHOULD IT EVER DIE?
DARLING, YOU AND I
ARE TOO WONDERFULLY HAPPY TODAY
TO THROW IT AWAY.
NOW, LIFE IS A SONG
IF WE BUILD A DUET ON IT,
HOW COULD WE BE WRONG?

(They are in a Paris apartment; he is in bed, watching her; she is in her undergarments, folding her clothes.)

    EVANGELINE. Good-bye Andre. And good riddance. You and Madeline can have each other. I've found someone new.

    ALEXI.
THE MOMENT I SAW YOU, AND YOU LOOKED MY WAY...

    EVANGELINE.
OH, HOW COULD WE BE WRONG?
COULD WE BE WRONG?
COULD WE BE WRONG?

End of Scene 4

Scene 5

Scene: *A Paris Street / Café.*
Time: *Several weeks later.*
At Rise: *Evangeline enters agitated, wearing the remains of what*
           looks to be a painting; she is yelling at someone off stage.

EVANGELINE. Well you cad, had you not been chasing me around, I would not have fallen through your painting. You unspeakable man. You charlatan, preying on helpless young women. *(Aside.)* Paris has not been pretty. Poor Alexi, and I do mean poor, is out of money and out of hope, I fear, of ever finding work. We haven't eaten in days. ~~That is why I agreed to pose in the nude for a so-called artist.~~ ~~*(Beat.)* But he turned out to be more panter than painter~~....

(Lights up on VICTOR sitting at a café table; he notices her and approaches.)

VICTOR. Oh, Miss. Miss, do you remember me?
EVANGELINE. Should I?
VICTOR. We met briefly and quite by accident in—
EVANGELINE. Neauville?
VICTOR. Lausanne. I killed your flower.

(He fumbles in his pocket and produces a bent, dog-eared, poor excuse of a dried rose. He shows it to her proudly.)

EVANGELINE. Of course. You are in the field of accounting.
VICTOR. Horticulture. ~~Smashing outfit, is that the latest rage in Paris?~~
EVANGELINE. ~~Oh, my God. I have to get out of this.~~ It's been swell seeing you again … Billy?
VICTOR. Victor! Listen, I'm in Paris a few days. Do you think we could spend some time—
EVANGELINE. That would be quite impossible. Please excuse me.
VICTOR. But I don't even know your name.
EVANGELINE. Evangeline. ~~Now, I must get home.~~
VICTOR. *(Watching her exit.)* Evangeline. ~~Home. What I wouldn't give~~....

MUSIC: YOU'D BE SO NICE TO COME HOME TO

VICTOR.
IT'S NOT THAT YOU'RE FAIRER

THAN A LOT OF GIRLS JUST AS PLEASIN'
THAT I DOFF MY HAT AS A WORSHIPPER AT YOUR SHRINE.
IT'S NOT THAT YOU'RE RARER
THAN ASPARAGUS OUT OF SEASON,
NO, MY DARLING, THIS IS THE REASON WHY YOU'VE GOT
    TO BE MINE.

YOU'D BE SO NICE TO COME HOME TO,
YOU'D BE SO NICE BY THE FIRE.
WHILE THE BREEZE ON HIGH SANG A LULLABY.
YOU'D BE ALL THAT I COULD DESIRE.

UNDER STARS CHILLED BY THE WINTER,
UNDER AN AUGUST MOON BURNING ABOVE,
YOU'D BE SO NICE, YOU'D BE PARADISE
TO COME HOME TO AND LOVE.

(Spot down on VICTOR. Blackout.)

End of Scene 5

Scene 6

Bed For Me
U/S

Scene: *The large apartment of Pierre Fort.*
Time: *Immediately following.*
At Rise: *Paintings fly in and a large statue comes center as party*
         guests in tight formation enter from one wing. Their backs
         are always to the audience; through dance and movement
         they consider the paintings and socialize.

(EVANGELINE and ALEXI enter from opposite sides.)

   ~~ALEXI. Ah, you got my note.~~
   EVANGELINE. *(Reading the note.)* 'Dear Evangeline, I was
about to kill myself when I remembered Pierre Fort is having a party
tonight. Meet me there.' Really, Alexi, this death wish of yours—
   ALEXI. These may be the worst paintings in all of Paris.
Where's the food?
   EVANGELINE. *(Examining the painting of a female nude.)*
This woman looks so familiar. I am sure I know her.
   ~~ALEXI. She might be prettier with just one nose.~~

(The formation of guests parts and Joyce, holding a plate of hors d'

oeuvres and dressed as a bohemian gypsy, moves DC. The group closes rank again and moves off. Seeing JOYCE, EVANGELINE does a double take.)

EVANGELINE. Joyce? Is it really you? ~~The painting! I was sure I knew that woman!~~

JOYCE. Vangy Darling! How fun running into you here. *(Considering her nude portrait.)* Don't I look fabulous darling? ~~Pierre, I think, has managed to capture my essence.~~ *(Eyeing ALEXI.)* This I take it would *not* be your dear Aunt Ermyntrude?

EVANGELINE. Joyce, I would like you to meet my dear friend Alexi Gregorgevitch Stukin.

JOYCE. *(Pulling EVANGELINE aside.)* Darling, he's Russian. How exciting. Is he a Communist?

EVANGELINE. Umm, more a pessimist I think. *(JOYCE hands EVANGELINE the hors d'oeuvres, which she devours. JOYCE, turning to ALEXI, offers her hand; he kisses it sensuously. The two of them make eyes at each other until EVANGELINE interrupts.)* Joyce, how did you end up in Paris?

JOYCE. Isn't it all too killing? I got back to England and the old Governor had run off with one of the chambermaids.

EVANGELINE. *(Aside to audience.)* Her father. She must have been devastated.

JOYCE. Needless to say, I was devastated. *(Beat.)* Until I thought, experiment! So, when I met Pierre at a party in London I decided to support the arts. Having no idea, that actually meant supporting Pierre, the lazy lout. *(Taking ALEXI by the arm.)* Come Alexi, let me show you ~~the other~~ paintings.

ALEXI. And the buffet?

JOYCE. You don't mind do you, Vangy? Of course you don't!

(JOYCE and ALEXI exit; EVANGELINE moves to the statue.)

EVANGELINE. *(To audience.)* She's changed. She used to be so unassuming. Imagine! Meeting Joyce in Paris. I guess Miss Pratt's words had some effect on all of us. God knows what Madeline is doing these days. *(MADELINE crosses upstage dressed in sweeping furs, admiring the diamond bracelets on her arm.)* She had begun to experiment long before she came to school. And it positively makes my knees weak to think what Henrietta may be up to. *(HENRIETTA crosses upstage with a wine skin tipped in her mouth.)* Or Bertha. No, Bertie I'm sure will end up a happy hausfrau with a whole herd of chubby, rosy-cheeked children. Her very own kindergarten. *(Bertha crosses upstage carrying lots of luggage.)* It seems, not so long ago, we were such innocents. And now, look at us, nymph errants, each off on an adventure. Each of us searching for that special something. *(From behind the statue, a German-looking man appears, holding a plate of hors d' oeurves; he clicks his heels and bows to EVANGELINE. She eyes the food, walks over to him and reaches for the plate.)* May I ?

FRTIZ. Please. Food is the only thing in this rotten city I can still stomach.

EVANGELINE. *(Chowing down.)* You don't care for Paris?

FRITZ. Here, I feel myself sodden with sex.

EVANGELINE. Well, if one has to be sodden with something— Oh, you were being serious.

(A girl doing an impression of Isadora Duncan leaps across the stage wearing little more than a flowing chiffon scarf. EVANGELINE and FRITZ observe; JOYCE enters and stands nearby, watching them.)

FRITZ. A transparent dentelle like that is the worst. It is lewd, suggestive and obscene.

EVANGELINE. Really! And I thought it was some sort of dance. Well, one simply can't go around without any clothes at all.

JOYCE. But Vangy, according to nature boy here, one must. Because, in his mind, only complete nudity is chaste. If you can imagine. I warn you, this one can bore you for simply hours and hours about the advantages of baring his soul, not to mention his body in the great outdoors.

EVANGELINE. But darling, I thought the great outdoors was what you so loved. Riding in the country, hunting.

JOYCE. That was fine for a schoolgirl, but all that has lost its allure. My new pastimes of choice are parties, city life and men! Hills and dales, you can have them. I now prefer the great *in*doors.

MUSIC: THE GREAT INDOORS

JOYCE.
WHEN THE WEEKEND COMES,
ALL MY DEAREST CHUMS
TO THE COUNTRY GO TEARING OFF,
TO IMPROVE THEIR FRAMES
PLAYING DAMN-FOOL GAMES
SUCH AS POLO AND TOM THUMB GOLF.
WHILE THEY'RE BREAKING GROUND,
BIFFING BALLS AROUND,
AND PERSPIRING TO BEAT THE BAND,
I AM SITTING PRETTY

IN THE GREAT BIG CITY,
WITH A COOL DRINK IN MY HAND.

FROM SATURDAY UNTIL MONDAY
I'M WHAT THE SPORTSMAN ABHORS,
A WEEKEND HATER
THANKING MY CREATOR
FOR THE GREAT INDOORS.
WHILE ALL THE OTHERS ARE RUSHING
FROM BATHING SUITS TO PLUS FOURS,
YOU'LL FIND THIS MAMMA'S STILL IN HER PAJAMAS'
FOR THE GREAT INDOORS. *Dialogue P.30*

THE BREEZE MAY DIE,
BUT WHAT CARE I,
I'VE GOT A BIG ELECTRIC FAN.
IF PASSING BY,
COME IN AND TRY
BITING YOUR INITIAL ON MY ARTIFICIAL TAN
INSTEAD OF WRECKING MY SYSTEM
BY PLAYING GAMES WITH OLD BORES,
I TAKE NO CHANCES,
SITTING ON MY FRANCES,
IN THE GREAT INDOORS.

JOYCE. *(Calling out.)* Alexi darling, help yourself to more food. *(Back to EVANGELINE.)* I love a man with a healthy appetite.

EVANGELINE. Joyce I should warn you about Alexi. You don't need his problems.

JOYCE. And I suppose you do. Vangy, I must tell you, as a friend, that Alexi feels misunderstood by you.

EVANGELINE, Why? Because I won't kill myself?

JOYCE. I am sure he has his reasons. As he was stuffing shrimp into his mouth—

EVANGELINE. He had shrimp?

JOYCE. At that very moment, I realized Pierre and I were finished. He never showed such passion. Not like Alexi. You should have seen the lusty way he devoured that turkey breast.

EVANGELINE. A turkey breast. The pig. Umm pig. What were you saying?

JOYCE. Alexi wants me. His feelings have nothing to do with my money. If you don't believe me— *(Calling out.)* Alexi it's me, not Evangeline you want to be with, isn't it, darling? *(A voice responds that sounds like someone talking with their mouth full.)* The attraction is so powerful that you want to move in with me as soon as Pierre packs his bags. Isn't that true, Alexi dear? *(This time, the off-stage response sounds like choking on food.)* I'm sorry you had to hear it like that Vangy. I do hope we can still be friends, because dear, *(Rushing off to ALEXI.)* you are my friend.

EVANGELINE. *(Turning to Fritz; trying to be brave.)* Well, that ends that. Just as well. He was becoming a danger to my health.

FRITZ. I am bound for Himmelheim. It is a beautiful nudist colony in the far north of Austria. There, unencumbered, I can freely walk among the pine trees and swim in the clear, blue lakes. Please, you will come as my guest.

EVANGELINE. Walking in the woods naked. I say, isn't that quite cold, you know, on your—

FRITZ. In the morning only. Soon, the sun comes out, and you are glowing with good health and warmth. What do you say?

EVANGELINE. I must be quite delirious from stress or lack of food because I'm thinking of saying yes. At least this time, having nothing to wear, seems appropriate. But I don't even know your name.

FRITZ. Fritz Tagendorfer.

EVANGELINE. Well Fritz, I confess, it would be nice to get away from so-called modern society.

MUSIC: BACK TO NATURE

EVANGELINE.
LET'S QUIT THIS WEARY WORLD OF OURS
AND LIVE AMONG THE BIRDS, THE FLOW'RS.
THE BUTTERFLIES, THE CRICKETS AND THE FROGS.
    FRITZ.
'T'WOULD BE A FAR MORE PLEASANT THING
THAN SITTING HERE AND WITNESSING *(The paintings fly out.)*
OUR CIVILIZATION GOING TO THE DOGS.
    EVANGELINE.
WHY, JUST REGARD THE HEADLINES
IN CASE YOU HAVEN'T READ.

(The set changes to a woodland setting. As the song progresses, they start removing their clothes; by the song's end, they are naked, but hidden by pieces of scenery.)

    FRITZ.
"IN BUCHAREST, THE BREAD LINES
HAVE ALL RUN OUT OF BREAD."
    EVANGELINE.
"THE PUBS THROUGHOUT GREAT BRITAIN
WILL ALL BE FORCED TO CLOSE."

FRITZ.
"OUR DELEGATE TO SWITZERLAND
COMES HOME WITH A BLOODY NOSE."
     EVANGELINE.
"TEN THOUSAND HEADS OF CHINESE BANDITS HANG HIGH.
IN THE CROWDED STREETS OF SHANGHAI."
     FRITZ.
"MARKET DROPS TO DOUBLE ZERO."
"GANGSTER MADE A NATIONAL HERO."
     EVANGELINE.
"ROYALISTS TURN BOLSHEVISTIC
BOLSHEVIKS TURN ROYALISTIC."
     FRITZ.
"WAR IN TIMBUKTU."
"SNAKES ESCAPED FROM LONDON ZOO."
     EVANGELINE.
"NO MORE COWS IN CHANNEL ISLANDS,"
"NO MORE GROUSE IN SCOTTISH HIGHLANDS."
     FRITZ.
"NO MORE COWBOYS ON THE PRAIRIES."
"IN THE BUSHES, NO MORE FAIRIES."
     EVANGELINE.
EV'RY MOMENT , FASTER, FASTER,
CLOSER, CLOSER, COMES DISASTER.
DARLING IF YOU LOVE ME, YOU'D BETTER TAKE ME
BACK TO NATURE WITH YOU.
     FRITZ.
BACK TO NATURE WE TWO.
WHAT A SHAKE-UP IN LIFE'S MONOTONY
     EVANGELINE.
DEAR, TO WAKE UP WITH YOU AND BOTANY.
     FRITZ.
OTHER MUSIC WE'LL BAN
FOR THE SWEET PIPES OF PAN.
     EVANGELINE.
AND WHEN NIGHT FALLS WITHOUT APOLOGY
YOU CAN GIVE ME A LESSON IN BIOLOGY.
     FRITZ.
FOR I SO WANT TO GO WHERE YOU DO,
BACK TO NATURE WITH YOU.

(Blackout.)

End of Scene 6

Scene 7

Scene: The Grand Hotel Kurzdorfer.
Time: A few days later.
*At Rise: Evangeline stands under a tight spotlight that shows only her
        face.*

EVANGELINE. *(To audience.)* I can hear you saying to yourselves, now what has happened to her! Well, everything was fine until
we had a picnic on the top of that blasted mountain. Suddenly, I find
myself in the altogether, and he wants to know why I seem uncomfort-
able. Then without so much as a how-do-you-do, he wanted to know if
we should enjoy the big sausage. I inquired if he wouldn't like to have
lunch first. Imagine my surprise when I looked over and he was actually putting a knockwurst on the fire. Then there was the trouble with
the snow. Being of a practical nature, I grabbed the only thing I could
find to give some warmth and created this fetching ensemble. *(Spot
widens; she is wearing a bright, checked picnic tablecloth)* Knowing
Fritz's feelings about clothes, I should have realized there would be
trouble. Upon seeing me, like so, he dropped the firewood, completely
smashing his big sausage. Completely seduced, he came after me like
some barbaric Neanderthal. The only thing I could think of was to
run. And run I did. I lost him in a meadow when he stubbed his toe on
a large rock. Now, I've walked twenty kilometers to this hotel. And—
What am I going to do?

MUSIC: EXPERIMENT (STING)

EVANGELINE. Oh shut up! Experiment! So far it's brought me
a cheating Frenchman, a mad Russian and a nasty nude German.

*(Lights up on an ornate grand hotel lobby. A young man is on the
    phone, his back to the audience. EVANGELINE passes him, exit-
    ing just as he turns.)*

VICTOR. *(Into the phone.)* You'll be happy to know I've saved
their shrubbery. Yes, the hotel manager seemed quite appreciative.
But I tell you, I must get back to Paris. That was where I last saw her.
No, you don't understand. I wish I could get her out of my mind. But I
can't. This may sound crazy. I barely know her, but I know I love her.
Find me work there. Please. She is the most important thing in my
life.

(He hangs up the phone and pulls out a bent, dried rose, the keepsake

that reminds him of EVANGELINE.)

MUSIC: YOU'RE TOO FAR AWAY

VICTOR.
I READ SO MANY TALES OF LOVE
I DIDN'T B'LIVE THEM TRUE
UNTIL THE DAY WHEN HEAV'N ABOVE
FIRST LET ME GAZE AT YOU.
SO I SUPPOSE IT'S LOVE'S REVENGE
THAT I SHOULD LONG SO MUCH
FOR ONE SO FAIR, SO RARE,
BUT ONE I DARE NOT TOUCH.

I THINK OF YOU AND SUDDENLY START
TO SING YOU THE SONG THAT'S BEEN LONG IN MY HEART.
I SING IN VAIN
YOU'RE TOO FAR AWAY.
WHY SHOULD I DREAM OF WONDERFUL NIGHTS
WHEN I'M IN THE DEPTHS DEAR, AND YOU'RE ON THE
    HEIGHTS?
IT'S ALL SO PLAIN,
YOU'RE TOO FAR AWAY.

I ONLY PINE TO MAKE YOU MINE.
BUT EV'RY MOMENT IT'S CLEARER
THAT I CAN'T SUCCEED TILL YOU'VE AGREED
TO COME JUST A LITTLE BIT NEARER.

AND TILL WE'RE SO CLOSE TOGETHER THAT WE
CAN'T TELL ANY LONGER WHAT'S YOU AND WHAT'S ME,
I'LL STILL MAINTAIN
YOU'RE TOO FAR AWAY.

(At the end of the song, VICTOR sniffs the rose as he exits; EVANGELINE backs on-stage, still wearing her tablecloth.)

EVANGELINE. *(To someone off-stage.)* There really is no need for you to be so rude. I'm well aware that I have no luggage, identification or money. But do I look like a vagrant? Don't you worry about me loitering in your precious lobby. I'll be gone soon enough. Oooh! *(Turning to audience.)* What a perfectly horrid little clerk. Well, here is a new twist in my adventures. It wasn't until this moment that I realized I have never traveled alone. What a quandary. On the one hand, I am *not* about to go back up that mountain and freeze my flesh for Fritz. On the other hand, I seem to have no place to stay and nothing to eat. But at least, I still have my dignity. *(She walks over to a kiosk displaying rail timetables; she picks one up, reading and crying at the same time.)* Kurzdorf, Vienna, Frankfurt, Cologne, Paris— *(A hand appears from behind the kiosk offering her a handkerchief.)* Thank you. Calais, London— *(Realizing that someone has handed her the handkerchief.)* Oh!

COUNT. *(Stepping out from behind the kiosk.)* Why the tears? Whatever it is, I am sure there is a simple solution. Permit me. I am Joseph Ferdinand Leopold von Hohenadelborn-Mantalini, Furst von und zu Hohenadelborn, Principe della Bocca Grande del Po, Count of the Holy Roman Empire, Chevalier of the Order of the Golden Fleece, Knight of the Order of the Crown of Tuscany, recently abolished, and Knight of the Order of the Golden Eagle of Bohemia, twice removed. My friends call me Count Ferdinand.

EVANGELINE. Evangeline.

COUNT. What a pretty name! Tell me Eve Angeline, do you like this hotel?

EVANGELINE. *(Looking off to desk clerk.)* Frankly, I think the service leaves much to be desired.

COUNT. May I offer you a lift somewhere?

EVANGELINE. That would be such a help. Where are you going?

COUNT. Venice. To attend a party in honor of my friend, Constantine Koumoudouropolos.

EVANGELINE. The shipping magnate?

COUNT. The very one. The party is at my palazzo, which I've rented. While there, I intend to sell the property.

EVANGELINE. A party in Venice? It sounds lovely! And given my present circumstances, I really don't see that I can—

COUNT. *(Cutting her off.)* Then Venice it is. And along the way, we shall stop and find you some proper clothes. I'll tell the driver to bring the car around and meet us in front.

(When she nods, he turns and exits; she primps in front of a lobby mirror.)

EVANGELINE. What a refined, distinguished man. What a catch. After all the recent boys in my life, how refreshing. This trip to Venice should be lovely. He will get to know me, I will get to know him. And who knows, perhaps he's the one. And royalty, no less. Wouldn't that be a shocker? There was obviously something that he saw in me. In my bearing. Not the Fritz kind of baring, mind you. I mean the way that I carry myself. Yes, the poise that shines even through adversity. That's what must have caught his regal attention. Well, Madeline old girl, if you could only see me now. I would stack my count against your producer any day. Never find my prince charming indeed. Ha!

(VICTOR enters carrying a suitcase; seeing her, his mouth drops.)

VICTOR. Evangeline, is it really you?

EVANGELINE. *(Turning and regarding him.)* You. You — I know who you are.

VICTOR. I can't believe my luck. That you are here. That I've found you.

EVANGELINE. Have you been following me?

VICTOR. I wish I had in Paris. I was on my way back there to look for you. But you're here. That dress, is it another of those latest rage things?

EVANGELINE. Yes, it's something I envisioned in the great outdoors. I call it woodland chic. *(Pushing past him.)* Now, if you will excuse me. I'm off to Venice.

VICTOR. Venice? You can't go to Venice!

EVANGELINE. Oh, really! And exactly who are you to tell me what I can and can not do?

VICTOR. I think I lo...lo...like you.

EVANGELINE. Like? You're such a boy! *(There is the honking of a car.)* Now, if you don't mind, there is a real gentleman waiting for me. *(Turning just before she exits.)* And stop following me, you're becoming obsessive.

VICTOR. Evangeline please, wait —

(He looks in her direction; there is the sound of a car motoring away.)

MUSIC: YOU'RE TOO FAR AWAY / REPRISE

VICTOR.
I ONLY PINE TO MAKE YOU MINE
BUT EV'RY MOMENT IT'S CLEARER
THAT I CAN'T SUCCEED TILL YOU'VE AGREED
TO COME JUST A LITTLE BIT NEARER.
AND TILL WE'RE SO CLOSE TOGETHER THAT WE
CAN'T TELL ANY LONGER WHAT'S YOU AND WHAT'S ME,
I'LL STILL MAINTAIN
YOU'RE TOO FAR AWAY.

(As Victor exits, the hotel lobby tracks out and the hallway of a Venetian palazzo flies in.)

End of Scene 7

Scene 8

Scene: *A palazzo in Venice.*
Time: *A few days later - evening.*
At Rise: *A drop flies in of a long hallway. Maids enter, cleaning with*
        brooms and dust rags. HENRIETTA, dressed in white tie and
        tails, is followed by her mother.

MUSIC: THEY'RE ALWAYS ENTERTAINING

MAIDS.

Inser dialogue [handwritten]

RUN, RUN, RUN, RUSH
MOP, DUST, SWEEP, BRUSH.
WORK, WORK, WORK, UNTIL YOU DROP
ALL DAY, ALL NIGHT,
NO SLEEP IN SIGHT,
DIO MIO, WHEN WILL IT EVER STOP?
SINCE THE FAM'LY OF AMERICANS HAVE TAKEN THIS
    PALAZZO.
WE WORK SO HARD THAT EV'RYONE IS PRACTICALLY
    PAZZO.
YET WHEN WE SUGGEST
WE NEED A LITTLE REST,
THEY LOOK AT US AND LAUGH AT US AND SAY TO US,
"IS THAT SO?"
THEY'RE ALWAYS ENTERTAINING,
THESE AMERICANS WHO COME TO TOWN
FOREVER ENTERTAINING
IT'S NO WONDER WE'RE A BIT RUN DOWN.
EV'RY DAY THEY ASK A BUNCH
OF CELEBRITIES FOR LUNCH.
IF YOU THINK THAT THAT IS ALL,
EV'RY NIGHT THEY GIVE A BALL.
SO EXCUSE US FOR COMPLAINING,
BUT THESE AMERICANS ARE ALWAYS ENTERTAINING.

HENRIETTA. Mother, how many times do I have to say it: I don't give a hair ball who's invited.

(The COUNT and EVANGELINE enter; she is wearing a stunning gown.)

MOTHER. Count Ferdinand. So delighted you could join us.
COUNT. Madame Bamberg, a pleasure. May I introduce Miss

Eve Angeline Edwards. She wished to see the palazzo, so I took the liberty—

MOTHER. *(Insincere.)* How nice of you to accompany the count. Such an unexpected pleasure.

HENRIETTA. Evangeline? Can it be you?

EVANGELINE. Henrietta? *(Aside to audience.)* Are there words to convey the surprise? I think not!

HENRIETTA. Mama, this is Evangeline. We were at school together.

MOTHER. Really? And now look. Talk about graduating to bigger and better things. Where, may I ask, are you staying?

COUNT. We are at the same hotel, the Danieli.

MOTHER. Convenient. Henrietta, where are your manners? You haven't greeted the count.

COUNT. Hello, Henrietta. I trust you and your mother find the accommodations suitable.

HENRIETTA. What's not to like? It's a swell joint.

EVANGELINE. So, you and your mother are the tenants.

COUNT. With a very favorable option to buy. Now, where's my old friend, Constantine?

MOTHER. *(Taking the count by the arm and leading him off.)* In the drawing room. And there are certain matters we should discuss on the way.

HENRIETTA. *(Indicating the pin on her lapel.)* Evie, look. The woman in shining armor. The pin you gave me. I wear it always.

EVANGELINE. I seem to have lost mine.

HENRIETTA. Wear this one. From one nymph errant to another. Just for the evening. I insist. *(Removing the pin and attaching it to EVANGELINE's gown.)* There. The perfect accessory for someone traveling in such rarefied circles. Arriving with the count. And later, I am sure you will captivate Constantine.

EVANGELINE. I've heard his name mentioned in the news. What is he like?

HENRIETTA. Portly. Greek. A little rough around the edges, but all man. *(Pointing.)* See that big ship in the harbor? That's his yacht. He's worked for his wealth. Not like so many of these easily bruised blue-bloods that mama continually courts on my behalf. I don't mean the count. He's nice enough.

EVANGELINE. To tell the truth, I don't know him that well. But we seem to get along. *(Watching HENRIETTA adjust her bow tie.)* Why are you dressed like that? In a man's tie and tails?

HENRIETTA. Oh, well Constantine is mad about classical music. So, tonight's party is mama's masterpiece, a Chopin party. And, if you'll remember from those boring history lectures, Chopin was involved with a famous woman writer. Remember, she used a man's name and dressed like a man. So, I've come to the party—

EVANGELINE. As George Sand. ~~The outfit looks very smart on you. But what do you think that woman's real name was?~~

~~**HENRIETTA.** I don't know. Georgia?~~

MUSIC: GEORGIA SAND

HENRIETTA.
GEORGIA SAND WAS AN AUTHORESS
WHO, ALL THROUGH HER LIFE, HAD GREAT SUCCESS,
NOT ONLY WITH HER BOOKS
BUT ALSO WITH HER LOOKS.

(EVANGELINE takes a seat and watches.)

AMONG THE BOYS WHO GAVE HER FUN
YOUNG ALFRED DE MUSSET WAS THE ONE
THAT GEORGIA LOVED THE MOST,
FOR HE WAS SUCH A GOOD HOST.

EV'RY NIGHT THAT BEAU OF GEORGIA'S
GAVE AN AFFAIR THAT WOULD SCARE THE BORGIAS,
FRENCH CHAMPAGNE AND RUSSIAN BALLETS,
ELLINGTON'S BAND AND RUDY VALLEE'S.
ALL WENT RIGHT TILL ONE FINE NIGHT
HER FAVORITE OF MALES
GAVE A BALL AND, TO SHOCK THEM ALL,
GEORGIA CAME IN TAILS.
WHEN HE SAW HIS BEST GIRL IN TROUSERS,
ALFRED NEARLY DIED.
AND IN FRONT OF ALL THOSE CAROUSERS,
ALFRED LOUDLY CRIED:

GEORGIA SAND, DRESSED UP LIKE A GENT,
GEORGIA SAND, WHAT DO YOU REPRESENT?
WHERE ARE YOUR FRILLS
THAT GAVE ME SUCH THRILLS?
WHERE ARE THOSE UNDIES
THAT MADE MY SATURDAYS-TO-SUNDAYS?

GEORGIA SAND, CAN'T YOU UNDERSTAND
THOUGH I WORSHIP YOU

YOU'RE A LITTLE TOO
PLUMP, I FEAR

TO PULL A MARLENE DIETRICH, DEAR.
GEORGIA SAND, GO HOME AND CHANGE.

(Through scrim, framed pictures appear, each containing a frozen
  Dietrich-like dancer in tie and tails. The Dietrichs unfreeze and
  dance in their frames along with HENRIETTA. The faces of the
  dancers are unrecognizable, obscured by the scrim and lighting.)

HENRIETTA / GIRLS.
WHERE ARE YOUR FRILLS
THAT GAVE ME SUCH THRILLS?
WHERE ARE THOSE UNDIES
THAT MADE MY SATURDAYS-TO-SUNDAYS?

GEORGIA SAND, CAN'T YOU UNDERSTAND
THOUGH I WORSHIP YOU
YOU'RE A LITTLE TOO
P.L.U.M.P., I FEAR
TO PULL A MARLENE DIETRICH, DEAR.
GEORGIA SAND, GO HOME AND CHANGE.

(At the end of the number, the dancing Dietrichs turn back into
  the framed pictures. EVANGELINE enthusiastically applauds
  HENRIETTA as MADAME BAMBERG enters and motions to her
  daughter.)

HENRIETTA. Excuse me, Evangeline. When mama calls, I
must answer.

(HENRIETTA and her mother withdraw upstage; by their body lan-
  guage, they are having an angry, intense argument;
  EVANGELINE observes.)

EVANGELINE. *(Aside to audience.)* Henrietta appears none too
happy.
MOTHER. *(Following HENRIETTA downstage).* Henrietta, you
will listen to me, and you will obey. Since the day you were born, it
has been my dream for you to attain a title and become a lady. The
time has come. And that is that. *(Turning soft and moving closer to
HENRIETTA.)* Rely on mama to know best, dear. It will all work out
just the way it should.

(She tries to give HENRIETTA a kiss. When it is refused, she exits.)

HENRIETTA. I hate her, and I hate this life.

EVANGELINE. What happened?

HENRIETTA. The Count is short of funds, so Mother takes the Villa off his hands, and he takes me off hers. Whether I like it or not, I am going to be married. To the count.

(EVANGELINE looks devastated as the news sinks in. HENRIETTA breaks into tears and runs off; the count comes in behind EVANGELINE.)

COUNT. I hope you are not disappointed in Venice?

EVANGELINE. No, not in Venice.

COUNT. To me these places are all so familiar, but I found a new pleasure seeing them through your eyes. I don't know how to tell you. I hardly expect you to understand. I have lost you.

EVANGELINE. I know.

COUNT. What? You know?

EVANGELINE. That you have arranged for Henrietta to be your wife.

COUNT. Oh, that. No, this marriage would have changed nothing between us. We could still have continued on, but—

EVANGELINE. Then what exactly did you mean by saying you had lost me?

COUNT. The gambling, it is in my blood. Constantine and I began to play ecarte. I lost heavily, very heavily. Constantine offered to forego all his winnings if I would stake just one thing on the turn of a card. That one thing was you.

EVANGELINE. Me? Why, I've never even met the man.

COUNT. He saw us arrive. You are young, beautiful and new. He likes new. At any rate, I turned up the Queen of Hearts; Constantine, the Ace of Diamonds.

EVANGELINE. What does that mean? I am now Constantine's property? Not bloody likely!

COUNT. Naturally, I cannot compel you to accept the bargain, but I promised, as a man of honor, to try and persuade you. To go with him.

EVANGELINE. And a man of honor, such as you, must keep his word. *(Aside to audience.)* No matter where we go, we women don't seem to get too far. We're still nothing more than the pot in a game of cards. Honor? Rubbish. More like buying and selling. *(Shouting to the world.)* Look everyone a sale! Startling reductions!

COUNT. I am sincerely sorry. You have every right to be upset. I will tell Constantine —

EVANGELINE. You will tell Constantine, yes! I just want to get out of Venice. You're so good at arrangements, please arrange to have my things, the other clothes you purchased for me, sent to his yacht. It might be awkward cruising the Aegean in just one evening dress.

(The COUNT nods, bows and exits.)

MUSIC: NYMPH ERRANT

EVANGELINE.
MEN,
I USED TO TAKE YOU SO SERIOUSLY.
THEN,
I DREAMED ABOUT YOU DELIRIOUSLY.
BUT NOW I'VE COME SO FAR
I KNOW HOW HARMLESS YOU ARE,
SO I'M OFF TO FOLLOW THE VOICE
THAT WHISPERS MYSTERIOUSLY.

NYMPH ERRANT, GO WANDERING ON,
YOU'VE LIVED AND LEARNED
YOUR ILLUSIONS ARE GONE.
NYMPH ERRANT, FORGET YOUR BLUES,
YOU'VE ALL TO GAIN,
AND YOU'VE NOTHING TO LOSE;

SO CLIMB THE HILL
AND CROSS THE DALE,
LIKE THE PALE MOON ABOVE
AND GO SAILING GAILY ON AND ON AND ON,
FOREVER ON AND ON —
LAUGHING AT LOVE.

(The lights take on a dream-like quality, MADELINE, HENRIETTA, JOYCE and BERTHA in a surrealistic dream version of how we saw them in the first scene begin to dance around EVANGELINE.)

EVANGELINE / GIRLS.
NYMPH ERRANT, GO WANDERING ON,
YOU'VE LIVED AND LEARNED
YOUR ILLUSIONS ARE GONE.
NYMPH ERRANT, FORGET YOUR BLUES,
YOU'VE ALL TO GAIN,
AND YOU'VE NOTHING TO LOSE;

(On this last verse, the center doors open; CONSTANTINE stands in the frame, beckoning to EVANGELINE. The COCOTTE enters,

*beckoning to EVANGELINE. Turning to and then away from
each one, EVANGELINE straightens her shoulders and looks at
CONSTANTINE. She removes the pin of the knight on her gown
and throws it to the floor.)*

SO CLIMB THE HILL
AND CROSS THE DALE,
LIKE THE PALE MOON ABOVE
AND GO SAILING GAILY ON AND ON AND ON,
FOREVER ON AND ON—
LAUGHING AT LOVE.

*(On the very last line, tears streaming down her face, EVANGELINE
crosses to CONSTANTINE and takes his hand. He leads her out
as the girls look up stage reaching in vain for her. As the lights
fade to black, there are pin spots on a stricken EVANGELINE
and the COCOTTE, who is laughing with diabolical delight.)*

CURTAIN / END OF ACT I

ACT II

Scene 1

Scene: Ruins of a Grecian palace on the outskirts of Smyrna.
Time: A fall evening.
At Rise: At end of Entre Act, lights up on a group of tourists trudging through ruins. They are completely disheveled and look beaten into the ground.

MUSIC: RUINS

CHORUS.
RUINS, RUINS, RUINS
EV'RYWHERE WE GO THEY SHOW US RUINS,
WE SAW A PILE IN CARTHAGE,
IN ROME, ANOTHER LOT,

WHILE HERE, APART FROM THE BUGS AND FLEAS,
THE ONLY THING THEY'VE GOT
IS RUINS, RUINS, RUINS.
THEY CONSTITUTE OUR EVERY DAILY DOIN'S.

WE'RE OFF AGAIN, THANK HEAVEN,
NEXT AFTERNOON AT FOUR,
TO SAIL ACROSS THE WATER
TO EGYPT'S BALMY SHORE.

AND WHEN WE GET TO LUXOR
WE'LL BE DRAGGED TO SEE SOME MORE
RUINS, RUINS, RUINS

(Lights up on EVANGELINE in an evening dress sitting on a broken pedestal. She holds a martini glass with a long cigarette holder.)

EVANGELINE. *(To audience, while music underscores.)* Darlings there you are. When last seen, I was aboard Constantine's yacht.

For the next several days, we sailed stopping at this or that odd place.
To me, it's all ancient history. Besides, I was still in shock thinking of
my own storied past.

MUSIC: RUINS (Continued)

EVANGELINE.
WHEN WE STARTED ON THIS MEDITERRANEAN CRUISE
HE WAS QUITE PREPARED TO SQUANDER EV'RY RUPEE
ON THE KIND OF FUN ONE'S CLERGYMAN TABOOS.
THAT DELIGHTFUL SPORT THAT'S KNOWN AS MAKING
    WHOOPEE.

YET THOUGH STILL ATHIRST FOR RIBALD ARABIAN NIGHTS
I'M BECOMING SO DEPRESSED YOU WOULDN'T KNOW ME.
FOR WHENEVER I GET OUT TO SEE THE SIGHTS,
INSTEAD OF ANYTHING GAY— HE ALWAYS SHOWS ME
RUINS, RUINS, RUINS
EV'RYWHERE WE GO HE SHOWS ME RUINS,

*(CONSTANTINE's head pops up out of a stone chamber; music
    vamps under.)*

CONSTANTINE. Evangeline, I think I may have found a sarcophagus.
EVANGELINE. Lovely darling, why don't you just lie down in
there and get some rest. Visit with your ancestors. Whatever. *(Back to
audience.)* He just loves exploring. And what does he loves exploring? You guessed it.

MUSIC: RUINS (Continued)

EVANGELINE.
RUINS, RUINS, RUINS
EV'RYWHERE WE GO HE SHOWS ME RUINS,

EVANGELINE / CHORUS.
WE'RE OFF AGAIN, THANK HEAVEN,
NEXT AFTERNOON AT FOUR,
TO SAIL ACROSS THE WATER
TO EGYPT'S BALMY SHORE,

AND WHEN WE GET TO LUXOR
WE'LL BE DRAGGED TO SEE SOME MORE
RUINS, RUINS, RUINS.
RUINS, RUINS
    EVANGELINE.
WHERE'S THE YACHT!

(As the chorus straggles off on applause, EVANGELINE raises her glass.)

EVANGELINE. Here's to you, Miss Pratt. I've followed your directive to the letter, and look what I've achieved! My love life reduced to rubble here in the city of Smyrna. *(She downs her martini and reaches for a nearby container; it is empty.)* ~~Constantine — Now, where did he go?~~

(She approaches the sarcophagus and looks inside, but he is gone. Suddenly, CONSTANTINE's head pops up above a headless statue of the goddess Venus; EVANGELINE, seeing him, jumps.)

CONSTANTINE. Evangeline, you must come see this. Behind me, intact, is part of the entrance entablature.
EVANGELINE. I've had quite enough of facades, thank you. *(Aside to audience.)* Architectural and otherwise.
CONSTANTINE. But there is this beautiful carved relief —
EVANGELINE. Speaking of relief, darling, the martini shaker is empty, and I could really use another drink. *(There is a loud explosion and a flash of light from off stage.)* Is there a storm approaching? *(There is the sound of another explosion, then another.)* Over there, in the distance, the sky is lighting up. Constantine, what is going on?
CONSTANTINE. It is the Greek army attacking. At last, they have those Turkish dogs on the run. Now business will improve. For years, they have hindered my trade with their taxes and meddling.

(Another explosion goes off; this time, much closer.)

EVANGELINE. You brought me to a war?
CONSTANTINE. There is no need to worry. The Greeks have everything —

(An explosion rocks the stage; they each dive behind a pillar.)

EVANGELINE. Under control?

CONSTANTINE. That was a little close. *(The sky starts turning red. He jumps up and runs to her side.)* The city is burning! Come, quickly. I must check my warehouse.

EVANGELINE. *(Aside to audience.)* Right, don't worry about the English girl being blown to bits. Save the carpets! *(To CONSTANTINE.)* Shouldn't we return to the yacht immediately and get out of here?

CONSTANTINE. First, the warehouse. It's close to the harbor. I won't be long I promise.

EVANGELINE. Well, you can leave me off at the nearest bar on the way. *(Aside to audience.)* If a girl has to sit through a siege, she should at least be fortified with a good, stiff drink.

CONSTANTINE. *(Taking her by the hand.)* This way.

(As they exit, explosions continue and the sky lights up; a tavern set tracks on. In shadow, a woman, standing with her back to the audience, looks out a window. The door of the tavern opens and EVANGELINE stands in the entrance. She turns back to the street.)

EVANGELINE. Yes, go to your precious warehouse. I'll wait here. And please hurry. *(Entering, looking about.)* Not exactly the Ritz. *(Sitting down, addressing the woman at the window.)* Excuse me, yoo hoo, over here.

(The woman turns; she steps forward into the light; it is BERTHA.)

BERTHA. Evangeline?

EVANGELINE. *(Gasping and jumping up at the sight of her old school pal.)* Bertha in a taverna in Smyrna? *(Aside to audience.)* Can you honestly say you're surprised? *(To BERTHA.)* The last time we were together, you were heading off to University in Berlin.

BERTHA. Ja, and I did. Look, I still have the pin you gave me. Remember the quest for true love we talked of going on?

EVANGELINE. *(Aside to audience.)* Why does that sound familiar?

BERTHA. I did not need to quest, because love, it found me. In Herr Otto Vigler, my Professor of Economics. And to Smyrna we came. To get away from it all.

EVANGELINE. For that, Smyrna is certainly the place.

BERTHA. Teaching for him was kaput. He wanted to become a silk merchant. And I was his helper. It was wunderbar. Till he came down with the local fever. One evening he went for a walk. And never came back. That was weeks ago. Now, with the Greeks and Turks at war, what's become of my Otto, who knows. *(She goes to the bar and, reaching underneath, comes up with a pile of different colored pieces of silk.)* All that is left are these samples. Oh, this will be lovely with your dress. *(She hands the piece to EVANGELINE and, crying, puts the rest back.)* When he walked out, I had no money, no food, no way of going home. So, here you find me, working at this miserable tavern.

    EVANGELINE. Oh, you poor thing. ~~And he was your very first~~ love. I know what that's like.

    BERTHA. Ja, I remember when we were at school, you were how you say, crazy mad about some doctor. What happened there?

    MUSIC: THE PHYSICIAN

    EVANGELINE.
ONCE I LOVED SUCH A SHATTERING PHYSICIAN,
QUITE THE BEST-LOOKING DOCTOR IN THE STATE.
HE LOOKED AFTER MY PHYSICAL CONDITION,
AND HIS BEDSIDE MANNER WAS GREAT.

WHEN I'D GAZE UP AND SEE HIM THERE ABOVE ME,
LOOKING LESS LIKE A DOCTOR THAN A TURK,
I WAS TEMPTED TO WHISPER, "DO YOU LOVE ME,
OR DO YOU MERELY LOVE YOUR WORK?"

HE SAID MY BRONCHIAL TUBES WERE ENTRANCING
MY EPIGLOTTIS FILLED HIM WITH GLEE,
HE SIMPLY LOVED MY LARYNX
AND WENT WILD ABOUT MY PHARYNX,
BUT HE NEVER SAID HE LOVED ME.
HE SAID MY EPIDERMIS WAS DARLING,
AND FOUND MY BLOOD AS BLUE AS COULD BE,
HE WENT THROUGH WILD ECSTATICS,
WHEN I SHOWED HIM MY LYMPHATICS,
BUT HE NEVER SAID HE LOVED ME.

AND THOUGH, NO DOUBT,
IT WAS NOT VERY SMART OF ME,
I KEPT ON A-WRACKING MY SOUL
TO FIGURE OUT
WHY HE LOVED EV'RY PART OF ME,
AND YET NOT ME AS A WHOLE.

WITH MY ESOPHAGUS HE WAS RAVISHED,
ENTHUSIASTIC TO A DEGREE,
HE SAID 'T'WAS JUST ENORMOUS,
MY APPENDIX VERMIFORMIS,
BUT HE NEVER SAID HE LOVED ME.
HE SAID MY CEREBELLUM WAS BRILLIANT
AND MY CEREBRUM FAR FROM N.G
I KNOW HE THOUGHT A LOTTA
MY MENDULLA OBLONGATA,
BUT HE NEVER SAID HE LOVED ME.

HE SAID MY MAXILLARIES WERE MARVELS.
AND FOUND MY STERNUM STUNNING TO SEE,
HE DID A DOUBLE HURDLE
WHEN I SHOOK MY PELVIC GIRDLE,
BUT HE NEVER SAID HE LOVED ME.
HE SEEMED AMUSED
WHEN HE FIRST MADE A TEST OF ME
TO FURTHER HIS MEDICAL ART,
YET HE REFUSED
WHEN HE'D FIXED UP THE REST OF ME,
TO CURE THAT ACHE IN MY HEART

I KNOW HE THOUGHT MY PANCREAS PERFECT,
AND FOR MY SPLEEN WAS KEEN AS COULD BE.
HE SAID OF ALL HIS SWEETIES,
I'D THE SWEETEST DIABETES,
BUT HE NEVER SAID HE LOVED ME.
NO, HE NEVER SAID
NO, HE NEVER SAID HE LOVED ME

BERTHA. You kid me, ja? That was all he had to say?
EVANGELINE. Come to think of it ….

MUSIC: THE PHYSICIAN / ENCORE

EVANGELINE.
HE SAID MY VERTEBRAE WERE "SEHR SCHONE,"
AND CALLED MY COCCYX "PLUS QUE GENTIL,"
HE MURMURED MOTE BELLA
WHEN I SAT ON HIS PATELLA,
BUT HE NEVER SAID HE LOVED ME.
HE TOOK A FLEETING LOOK AT MY THORAX,
AND STARTED SINGING SLIGHTLY OFF KEY,
HE CRIED, "MAY HEAVEN STRIKE US,"

WHEN I PLAYED MY UMBILICUS,
BUT HE NEVER SAID HE LOVED ME.

AS IT WAS DARK
I SUGGESTED WE WALK ABOUT
BEFORE HE RETURNED TO HIS POST.
ONCE IN THE PARK,
I INDUCED HIM TO TALK ABOUT
THE THING I WANTED THE MOST
HE LINGERED ON WITH ME UNTIL MORNING,
YET WHEN I TRIED TO PAY HIM HIS FEE,
HE SAID, "WHY DON'T BE FUNNY,
IT IS I WHO OWE YOU MONEY,"
BUT HE NEVER SAID
NO, HE NEVER SAID,
NO, HE NEVER SAID HE LOVED ME.

*(There are explosions and gun shots; they cling to each other in fear.
BERTHA runs to the window; EVANGELINE puts the silk about
her neck.)*

BERTHA. There are fires and bodies in the street. The Turks are
taking over.
EVANGELINE. Where is he? What could be keeping him?
BERTHA. Keeping who?
EVANGELINE. Constantine Koumou—Koumadar—a Greek
gentleman. My escort. Now, when he returns, we will go straight-
away to his yacht in the harbor. And Bertha, you shall come with us.
We'll see that you get safely home.

*(There is another explosion, running footsteps, shouting and a
scream.)*

BERTHA. Your escort, is he a bit stocky?
EVANGELINE. Yes, with black hair.
BERTHA. And a mustache? Wearing a white suit?
EVANGELINE. That's him. Do you see him?
BERTHA. I don't think he will be coming back.

*(EVANGELINE goes to the window and is horrified by what she
sees.)*

EVANGELINE. No, no! Oh, Constantine, you tragic little man.
~~Like most men, all you wanted were old ruins and young women. Sad~~
~~yes, but not a crime.~~

*(The door bursts open and KASSIM, a rough and tumble Turkish sol-
dier wielding a sword, poses menacingly in the entrance way.)*

KASSIM, Ah, ha! Ha, ha, ha! The Turkish army has won. The
city is ours. I am Kassim, the victorious. And you are plainly fright-
ened. Cowering in fear like women.
BERTHA. We are women.

*(KASSIM advances; he turns on a lamp and squints, getting a better
look.)*

KASSIM. So you are. But that may not stop me from making a
shish kabob of you as I did that silly, stupid businessman in the street.

(He raises his fingers to his mouth and spits.)

EVANGELINE. You sir are quite disgusting!
KASSIM. You dare to speak to Kassim in this manner? *(He
grabs the scarf around EVANGELINE's neck and pulls her to him.
Distracted by the scarf, he suddenly becomes girlish and excited.)* Is
this silk?
EVANGELINE. Yes, don't you just love the feel against your
skin?

*(He puts the scarf on and parades around, arranging it in different
ways.)*

KASSIM. Very nice. Striking in fact. The way it offsets my
fierceness. You let me have? Wait, I don't ask. I take. Is mine. My
sword makes it so.
EVANGELINE. Yes, yes. There's no reason to threaten. Let's
try to be civilized, shall we? *(Glaring, KASSIM swings his sword and
slices a chair in half.)* It was just a suggestion. *(Taking another tact.)*
Kassim, darling. It is Kassim isn't it? We might see our way to giving
you all the silk you could ever want, if you could take us to the British
Consulate.
KASSIM. All the silk I want. In pretty colors? *(There is a huge
explosion; KASSIM runs to the window.)* Uh, oh! There goes the British Consulate. *(Looking at them.)* Now, what am I to do with you, the
pillaging will begin soon.
EVANGELINE. *(Aside to audience.)* I have never actually been
pillaged— *(Back to KASSIM.)* Can you get us out of here?
KASSIM. I don't know. If not, you will soon be serving the
Turkish army.
BERTHA. Oh, I'm very good at that. *(They both turn to look at*

her.) Since working here, I have learned much about serving meals. *(An inspiration.)* And my friend would also work hard at this.

EVANGELINE. *(Aside to audience.)* How kind of Bertie. Volunteering me to wait on a horde of savages. *(Back to BERTHA and KASSIM.)* No, no, no. If that's the case, we might as well sell ourselves into slavery.

KASSIM. Sell *yourself?* What would you do with the profits? Slaves cannot have money.

EVANGELINE. No, slaves cannot, but let's suppose if someone ... say *you* were the seller— *(Aside to audience.)* What am I saying?

KASSIM. Ah, ha! Kassim sell you. Kassim keep money. And you throw in extra silk, too. It is deal. Now, where is that silk?

BERTHA Come inside into the light. Let me show you [handwritten]

(BERTHA reaches under the bar and brings up the silk; a delighted KASSIM looks through it, holding up pieces for a reaction from the girls as lights go down to a pin on EVANGELINE. The tavern set begins to track off stage.)

EVANGELINE. Well, Madeline, he may be more princess than prince charming, but you have to admit the whole thing fairly reeks of adventure— *(Sniffing the air.)* Or something.

(As lights go out on EVANGELINE, drums begin to pound in an exotic rhythm. Blackout.)

End of Scene 1

Grale Hwem [handwritten]

Scene 2

Scene: *The desert and then the harem quarters of an Emir's Mideastern palace.*
Time: *A few days later.*
At Rise: *Drums are beating in an exotic rhythm as a blistering sun rises over dunes as far as the eye can see.*

(BERTHA enters first, lugging a trunk on her back and a couple of suitcases under her arms. She is followed by EVANGELINE, who has a parasol.

MUSIC: BACK TO NATURE (Underscoring in a minor key)

EVANGELINE. *(Aside to audience.)* When things calmed down

in Smyrna, Kassim carted us off to a slave market, where we were promptly purchased. Poor Bertha is still a bit sensitive that I sold for ten dinars more than she. She thought we would go by the pound. Fortunately, we both attracted the same customer. Some wealthy Grand Pooh-Bah Emir.

BERTHA. Water! I need water!

EVANGELINE. Don't fret dear. The next oasis can't be far.

BERTHA. Why is it me that must always carry the bags!

EVANGELINE. Well, darling, you are the one who let the camel wander off into the dunes. *(Aside to audience.)* First Otto deserted her, now the camel. I hope she doesn't take it personally. *(looks back, off stage.)* Kassim are you sure this is the right direction? *(KASSIM, draped in flamboyant, flowing silk leaps across the stage. Aside to audience.)* Barbaric in his behavior, but such a flair for color!

(BERTHA and EVANGELINE cross the stage and exit after KASSIM; a harem girl enters and begins to dance as the desert gives way to the opulent harem quarters of a Sultan-like palace.)

MUSIC: (BAD FOR ME) HAREM DANCE MUSIC

(From the opposite wing, a second harem girl appears and joins in. A third dancing harem girl enters down center. The girls are all veiled and unidentifiable. As they finish and lights go up, they assume reclining poses around the quarters. EVANGELINE and BERTHA enter wearing harem outfits. EVANGELINE also has horn-rimmed glasses and is knitting what seems to be a twenty-foot long sock that she drags behind her. BERTHA holds a hookah, from which she occasionally takes an opiated puff.)

BERTHA. Evangeline, all you do is knit. What are you trying to make?

EVANGELINE. I'm not quite sure actually. But you know what they say, busy hands— *(Watching as BERTHA takes a puff from the hookah.)* Bertha, you have become far too attached to smoking that pipe. I think it's distorting your perception.

BERTHA. That could be. I wish I was spending less time with it and more time with Ali.

EVANGELINE. *(Surprised.)* You mean, Ali, the one who checks on us and orders us about? That Ali? Well, I have news for you, Bertha. Ali is a eunuch. . . ,

BERTHA. Yes, that is the word. Unique. He is unique. Special. In his oh so manly way.

EVANGELINE. *(Aside to audience.)* Now, there is a fantasy. I will just let it go. As Ali himself, no doubt, once did.

(There is the sound of a gong; the harem girls rise and become excited.)

HAREM GIRLS. Ay....eeeeeeee....ay, ay, ay, ay, ay! Ay....eeeee....ahhhhhh!

(ALI, the head eunuch enters, holding his ears from the girls' cries.)

ALI. Silence, or I will have you whipped!

(The girls immediately become docile.)

EVANGELINE. *(Aside to audience.)* There's Ali now. Isn't he a charmer?

ALI. *(Clapping his hands three times.)* Quick, quick. Everyone. Gather around. *(Counting heads.)* Four hundred ten, four hundred eleven, four hundred twelve, four hundred thirteen, four hundred fourteen. Good. All wives, mistresses and slaves accounted for.

EVANGELINE. Excuse me, Ali. Those numbers. There are four hundred and fourteen women at the palace? I never realized—

ALI. Yes, many women. Many female chambers in many buildings. The master likes to keep you separate. Easier to handle that way.

BERTHA. *(Taking a puff from the hookah, eyeing ALI with longing.)* Isn't he a dream? Ooops, did I say that out loud?

ALI. What is wrong with her?

EVANGELINE. She was just thinking of the Emir. Even though, since coming here some three months ago, neither she nor I have seen him once.

ALI. He is a busy man. And often travels.

EVANGELINE. But surely not all the time. Is he so monstrous that he dare not show himself?

ALI. On the contrary, he is considered quite handsome.

EVANGELINE. Perhaps he does not like women.

ALI. Then, why all of you? No, he is just a methodical man who believes in taking everything in order. Including his women.

EVANGELINE. And where might I be in that order? Just out of curiosity.

ALI. *(Thinking.)* Some three hundred and fifty down the line.

EVANGELINE. Three hund— Why, I could be here for many more months if not years before he—

ALI. Yes, that is correct

EVANGELINE. ~~*(Aside to audience.)* Really, it's one thing to lose your virtue to a man. Quite another to lose your youth.~~ *(Back to ALI.)* I must say Ali, the master's method hardly sounds romantic.

ALI. But it is very efficient. I like you Miss Evangeline. Let me run and get list, I will try to bump you to the top.

(ALI exits in a hurry.)

EVANGELINE. Bertie, we have to get out of here.

BERTHA. There is no escape, the doors are locked, and why would I want to leave? I like having regular meals and a warm place to sleep. And I've grown fond of Ali. *(Patting the hookah.)* Not to mention my friend here.

EVANGELINE. What if I could get the key Ali keeps at his belt? Oh, Bertie, stay if you have to, but at least help me, won't you?

BERTHA. Of course, I'll help you. What do you want me to do?

(ALI returns with the list.)

EVANGELINE. Just follow my lead.

MUSIC: CAZANOVA (In a tango tempo)

(EVANGELINE grabs BERTHA, and they start to dance; ALI is fascinated.)

ALI. That is wonderful, what do you call it?

EVANGELINE. The tango. It's all the rage in Europe.

(EVANGELINE spins BERTHA out as she grabs ALI. It becomes a comic dance for three as EVANGELINE, with BERTHA's help, tries to get the large key ring attached at ALI's waist . Just as it is within her reach, ALI moves.)

ALI. Oh, Miss Evangeline, what fun. I must run and show the other eunuchs.

(He hurries off, practicing his steps as he goes.)

EVANGELINE. Drat! I was so close. Now what? *(Looking about, seeing her knitting, picking it up.)* Bertie, I'm going out the window.

BERTHA. Because of one little set back?

EVANGELINE. *(Tying one end of the knitting to a column.)* I shall use my knitting as a rope and lower myself to the street. *(Tossing the rest out the window.)* I think it will work. One last chance, dear Bertha. Come with me.

(There is the sound of a gong; EVANGELINE ducks behind the column; the three harem girls enter; BERTHA tries to block their view of the knitted length leading out the window, but they see it and become alarmed.)

HAREM GIRLS. Ay...ohhh....peh...la, la, la, la! Thala....kah.... ooooohhhhhh...ay, ay, ay, ay!

BERTHA. Enough! Behave yourselves. All right, which one of you left the knitting hanging out the window? Maybe you planned to use it to slip out of the palace and meet a man. Even though you've got a lord and master. Well, you should be ashamed. It's a good thing I got here first. Before you all did something regrettable. Why, if you are not careful, you could end up like the wives of King Solomon. *(Leading the harem girls away, gesturing to EVANGELINE.)* You don't know about them? Come down here, and I will tell you.

(On first note of intro, BERTHA takes a puff from the hookah and blows a big cloud of smoke. Evangeline climbs through the window and disappears).

MUSIC: SOLOMON

BERTHA.
SO-OLOMON HAD A THOUSAND WIVES
AND BEING MIGHTY GOOD, HE WANTED ALL O'THEM
TO LEAD CONTENTED LIVES:
SO HE BOUGHT EACH MAMMA A PLAT'NUM PIANO,
A GOLD-LINED KIMONO AND A DIAMOND-STUDDED HIS-
PANO
SO-OLOMON HAD A THOUSAND WIVES.

IN SPITE O'ALL HE GAVE'EM, THE WIVES OF SOLOMON
FOUND THEIR POPPA SLOW
AND FOR HER JAZZIN' EV'RY WIFE O'SOLOMON TOOK ON
A GIGOLO.
AND WHILE THEY PAMPERED THOSE WELL-BUILT HEROES
BY BUNCHIN' THEM AND LUNCHIN' THEM AND SUPPIN'
THEM AT CIRO'S
SO-OLOMON HAD NO PLACE TO GO.

(BERTHA heads toward the window and unties the length of knitting, letting it fall outside. There is an offstage crash; BERTHA looks out and gives her fallen friend a sheepish wave. BERTHA closes the window, making sure it is securely locked. Still singing, she picks up the knitting needles and wields them like the knives in

the song.)

SOON, SOL BEGAN TO MISS THOSE BABY DOLLS O'HIS
AND SENT HIS FAV'ORITE SPIES TO LOOK AROUND
AND WHEN HE HEARD THE LOWDOWN ON THOSE MOLLS
    O'HIS
HE SAID, "GO OUT AND HUNT THE WHOLE DARN TOWN
TILL YOU'VE FOUND YOUR MASTER A THOUSAND KNIVES,
I'M TIRED OF DOIN' THE TREATING FOR A THOUSAND
    CHEATING WIVES.
SO-OLOMON IS GONNA CUT THE WHOLE CROP DOWN."

SO SO-OLOMON SUMMONED HIS THOUSAND WIVES,
THEN SO-OLOMON PULLED HIS THOUSAND KNIVES
AND HE SLASHED THEIR GIZZARDS AND GASHED THEIR
    MUZZLES
TILL ALL THAT WAS LEFT OF THEM WAS A LOT OF JIGSAW
    PUZZLES.

THEN SLOWLY MOUNTING HIS ROYAL DAIS,
HE PICKED UP HIS MICROPHONE AND SAID, "ALL I GOTTA
    SAY IS
SO-OLOMON NO LONGER HAS A THOUSAND WIVES."

*(BERTHA puffs on her hookah, regarding the girls as the lights go
    down and the set begins to transition.)*

End of Scene 2

Scene 3

Scene: *Station platform of Gare St. Lazare, Paris.*
Time: *Several days later.*
At Rise: *Lights up on platform; sounds of a train coming into the
    station.*

CONDUCTOR. (*Voiceover.*) Madame, Monsieur, the Simplon
Express is now arriving Paris Gare St. Lazare.

*(EVANGELINE, wearing a man's topcoat over her harem outfit en-
ters; she turns and waves off-stage.)*

EVANGELINE. Merci, Francoise. *(Aside to audience as she models the coat.)* Imagine, a Frenchman nice enough to give me his coat. Have I been away that long? Last you saw me, I was sliding down a palace wall to freedom. I made my way into a town, there exchanging the various harem baubles and trinkets on me for transport by bus, boat and then the train. Which has, at last, delivered me to Paris.

(A man enters, head down, hurrying along runs into EVANGELINE, knocking her down. It is VICTOR.)

VICTOR. I am so sorry. I wasn't watching where I was— You.

EVANGELINE. You!

VICTOR. *(Helping her up.)* Evangeline. Fancy this. Amazing, actually. Running into you.

EVANGELINE. Running over me is more like it.

VICTOR. You're as beautiful as ever. Is what you're wearing—

EVANGELINE. If you comment on my outfit I swear I will scream.

VICTOR. *(Trying to make conversation.)* Have you been in Venice all this time?

EVANGELINE, No, my plans changed just a bit.

VICTOR. You know, I think of you. Often.

EVANGELINE. I think of me often, too. Now, if you will excuse me.

VICTOR. Why, Evangeline? Why is it every time we meet you are cool toward me? You never give me a chance. My feelings for you are completely honorable.

EVANGELINE. Look, you—

VICTOR. Victor.

EVANGELINE. You kill my flower, run me over, catch me at the most embarrassing moments. What do you want from me?

VICTOR. Just your love.

EVANGELINE. No, you don't. You want to own and control. That's all you men ever want. So, if that's the way it is, then I can be cold and callous, too.

VICTOR. I don't know who or what has made you feel this way. But whoever it is, I would like to throttle them. I swear to you in my case, it's not true.

EVANGELINE. *(As he moves closer, she holds up a hand.)* Stop! Not another step. word.

VICTOR. But, we're supposed to get married, have children, grow old together. Don't ask me why. I knew from the day I first saw you. Call it fate.

EVANGELINE. Fate. Well, what I'm feeling seems more like

hate.

VICTOR. *(Hurt and angry.)* Hate? Really? No, I think with you, it could be guilt, because you can't face where you've been and what you may have done with other men.

EVANGELINE. You bastard! I never want to see you again!

(Breaking into tears, she pushes past him and exits behind a pile of bags.)

VICTOR. See me again? Not on a bet. You know, you really are a rude, insufferable bi— God, I didn't mean that. Yes, I did! Oh— Bloody hell!

MUSIC: WHEN LOVE COMES YOUR WAY

~~VICTOR.~~ MADELINE + Girls

IF EVER TO YOUR WOE
LOVE COMES TO YOU ONE DAY,
REMEMBER WHAT I SAY:
I'VE LOVED, I KNOW
LOVE HATES THE SIGHT OF TEARS,
LOVE ONLY CARES FOR LAUGHTER,
SO SAVE YOUR TEARS TILL AFTER
LOVE DISAPPEARS.
WHEN LOVE COMES YOUR WAY
TAKE EV'RY BIT OF JOY YOU CAN BORROW.
BE CAREFREE, BE GAY,

(EVANGELINE quietly steps out, watching and listening.)

FORGET THE WORLD AND SAY GOOD-BYE TO SORROW,
SIMPLY LIVE FOR TODAY,
AND NEVER THINK AT ALL OF TOMORROW,
FOR JUST WHEN YOU ARE SURE THAT LOVE HAS COME TO
     STAY
THEN LOVE FLIES AWAY.

(Dejected, VICTOR throws down the remains of the flower he has kept all this time. He begins to leave, stops, mutters to himself, comes back, picks up the flower and exits. EVANGELINE moves center, watching him go.)

EVANGELINE. *(Taken aback and almost in tears by what she has heard.)* ~~I would really love to believe that you felt that way.~~ Maybe ~~you aren't~~ he isn't such a bad sort after all. *(Sitting on a bench.)* Oh

Victor why does everything have to be so complicated between us.
(As she notices a kiosk, the lights go up on it, revealing a large poster for the show "La Poitrines au Paris," starring MADELINE and produced by ANDRE DE CROISSANT; the poster features an image of MADELINE in feathers and jewels.) Oh my God! Madeline look at you. *(Aside to audience.)* The shameless hussy. *(A man walks out of the shadows)* Victor? Victor? Is that you?

ANDRE. Pardon Mademoiselle.

EVANGELINE. Andre de Croissant. First your poster and now you in the flesh. *(Aside to audience.)* Sometimes I feel like there are only seven people in this world.

ANDRE. Why, Evangeline, what a lovely surprise. It is so good to see you after all this time. The poster, you like? It makes Madeline look very, very—

EVANGELINE. Yes, very. "La Poitrines au Paris."

ANDRE. Tonight is the opening, and you must come as my guest. We can catch the first curtain.

EVANGELINE. But alas, I have nothing to wear.

ANDRE. *(Regarding her peculiar outfit.)* We will sit in my box. No one will see you.

EVANGELINE. Will Madeline, on stage, be able to see me?

ANDRE. Oh yes. I am sure she will be so surprised.

EVANGELINE. That my dear Andre may be the understatement of the decade!

(Blackout.)

MUSIC: FANFARE

(There is orchestration and a fanfare that one hears in a typical French follies show. Curtain opens on a lavish, multi-tiered set, with large feathered fans on each level. To music, the fans begin to move, revealing the shapely arms, legs and torsos of the showgirls behind them. The faces of the showgirls remain concealed. The fans weave and undulate in provocative unison. On a musical cue, they suddenly part and there, centered on the stairs is MADELINE in a follies costume that leaves very little to the imagination.)

VOICEOVER. Mesdames, Mademoiselles, Messieurs. Monsieur Andre de Croissant and the Le Folies de Paris proudly present Madeline in "La Poitrines au Paris."

MUSIC: SI VOUS AIMEZ LES POITRINES

MADELINE.
TRAV'LERS I'VE SEEN
SAY THE PRETTIEST POITRINES
(Spoken.) Do you know what Poitrines are?
ARE THE ONES YOU FIND IN POONA.

OTHERS THAN THESE
SAY THE BUXOM BALINESE
HAVE THE GREATEST GOONA-GOONA.
SPANIARDS MAINTAIN
THAT THE KIND YOU FIND IN SPAIN
ARE SO FAIR THAT EV'RY MAN TUMBLES.
WHILE NOT LONG AGO

(ANDRE and EVANGELINE enter a theatre box and take their seats.
ANDRE blows a kiss to MADELINE, who does a double take
upon seeing EVANGELINE.)

MADELINE.
A BOY IN EASTBOURNE I KNOW
SIMPLY RAVED ABOUT THOSE ON THE CRUMBLES.
CES BELLES POITRINES SAU-VAGE
MAY BE VERY FAIR PERCHANCE
BUT WHY SHOULD ONE VOY-AGE
WHEN THE BEST OF THEM ARE MADE IN FRANCE?

(MADELINE moves closer to the theatre box to get a better view.
EVANGELINE waves and smiles; MADELINE looks annoyed.)

MADELINE.
SI VOUS AIMEZ LES POITRINES
COME TO GAY PAREE
SI LEUR BEAUTE VOUS A-NIME
COME AND CALL ON ME.
I WILL SHOW YOU HOW DI-VEENE
PARISIENNES POI-TRINES REALLY ARE.
IF YOU PROMISE ME, YOU NAUGHTY BOY.
NOT TO GO TOO FAR.

SI VOUS VOULEZ D'LA TEN-DRESSE
ET D'LA VOLUPTE,
LET ME GIVE YOU MY AD-DRESSE
FOR A RAINY DAY.

AND WHEN ZAT FEELING COMES A-STEALING
YOU KNOW WHAT I MEAN?
MAIS OUI, MONSIEUR.
COME AND PLAY WIZ ME IN GAY PAREE.
SI VOUS AIMEZ LES POITRINES.

(MADELINE moves about the stage and gestures to the music while the focus shifts to ANDRE and EVANGELINE in the theatre box.)

ANDRE. *(Putting an arm around EVANGELINE.)* You know Evangeline, you should stay in Paris.
EVANGELINE. *(Removing his arm.)* Oh Andre, we have been down that road. And besides, you have Madeline now.
ANDRE. Yes, and I probably don't deserve her.
EVANGELINE. Funny, I was thinking there is probably no one you deserve more.

(He gives her a strange look and sits back; the focus returns to MADELINE as she goes into her big finish.)

MUSIC: *SI VOUS AIMEZ LES POITRINES* *(Continued)*

MADELINE.
AND WHEN ZAT FEELING COMES A-STEALING
YOU KNOW WHAT I MEAN?
MAIS OUI, MONSIEUR.
COME AND PLAY WIZ ME IN GAY PAREE.
SI VOUS AIMEZ LES POITRINES.

(At the end of the number, MADELINE takes a bow, glares at the theatre box and brusquely exits. As ANDRE and EVANGELINE rise, the set transitions and the two of them are backstage. MADELINE enters and goes to a dressing area; she begins to change, pretending not to see them.)

ANDRE. Madeline, look who I found.
MADELINE. *(Looking up, coolly regarding EVANGELINE.)* Oh, Evangeline, what a surprise. Now, that I'm a star, I just never know who or what will wander in from my past.
EVANGELINE. *(Aside to audience.)* I could tell right off, she was thrilled to see me. *(To MADELINE.)* Hello, Madeline.
MADELINE. Well, did you enjoy my performance?
EVANGELINE. It certainly was … revealing.
MADELINE. *(Looking EVANGELINE over.)* My goodness,

what happened to you? This dreadful ensemble. I remember you used to look somewhat presentable.

EVANGELINE. And I remember you used to be somewhat civil. Before that big head of yours began to swell even more.

ANDRE. *(Trying to make peace.)* Now girls, pull in your claws. Let's not upset this happy reunion.

EVANGELINE. I'm sorry, Madeline, that you see me as a threat.

MADELINE. A threat? I see nothing threatening here. Come Andre, I need you to help me get out of my costume.

ANDRE. I will be right there. *(An unhappy MADELINE regards them both, then storms off stage.)* You will stay in Paris awhile, no?

EVANGELINE. I think I need to be getting home to England.

ANDRE. If you stay, I will provide you an apartment of your own. We can see each other. Madeline need never know. I will shower you with every happiness. Think about it.

MADELINE. *(Off stage.)* Andre!

ANDRE. Coming!

(He squeezes EVANGELINE's arm sensuously and then exits after MADELINE; EVANGELINE turns and exits onto the street.)

EVANGELINE. *(To herself.)* Perhaps I should think of where I've been and where I'm going. Is it on to Oxford, or back into the arms of Andre? That would certainly give Madeline her comeuppance. Me doing to her what she did to me. Now, that has a certain charm. But first I think a good night's sleep and some decent clothes. *(Taking charm bracelet off her ankle and starting to exit.)* One last trinket Evangeline old girl. Now where can I unload this? *(Lights up on a jewelry shop which is in the process of being closed for the night.)* Maybe I can get enough for this to get me back to Oxford. *(EVANGELINE enters the shop. There is a woman bent down behind the counter.)* Excuse me. Do you purchase—*(The woman comes up; it is MISS PRATT.)* Miss Pratt?

PRATT. Do I know you? Oh, my goodness, Evangeline Edwards. Let me look at you. That outfit. Very Bohemian. No doubt you've been abroad.

EVANGELINE. *(Aside to audience.)* If only she knew. *(Back to PRATT.)* But what are you doing here? Why aren't you at the school?

PRATT. I decided to take some of my own advice and experiment. I always longed to run my own shop. So, here I am.

EVANGELINE. *(Presenting the ankle bracelet.)* I was hoping to sell this.

PRATT. *(Extremely interested.)* Evangeline, wherever did you get this? *(Winks at EVANGELINE, examines the bracelet.)* I can go as high as twenty thousand francs. *(Happily stunned, EVANGELINE is speechless. PRATT interprets this as resistance.)* All-right, thirty thousand. But that is my final offer.

EVANGELINE. No, no, that will be fine.

(PRATT pulls out a tin box and counts out a pile of money on the counter. EVANGELINE takes the cash and turns to go. She starts to cry.)

PRATT. Are you all right, my dear? There, there. No matter how bad the outlook, sometimes, we just have to let fate take a hand.

EVANGELINE. What did you say? About fate ?

PRATT. Well, it is the thing that takes us through life. For instance, you could be fated to marry a prince or a count——

EVANGELINE. *(Aside to audience.)* I think we can safely rule out a count.

PRATT. Or your fate may be to find a nice young man who will love you with all his heart. Is there such a young man?

EVANGELINE. I suppose there is, or was. But I'm not sure he's the young man. Especially now. After the way I've just acted and the things I've said, he has every reason to despise me.

PRATT. But love, my dear, defies reason. If he truly cares for you, he will be waiting. Run child. Don't end up alone because you were afraid to take a chance. Go. REPRISE ?

(EVANGELINE takes the cash and reaches over and kisses Pratt on the cheek. She exits in one direction as ANDRE rushes in from the other. PRATT turns to him.)

PRATT. I am sorry Mousieur, but we are closed.

ANDRE. Please you must help me. I need a gift quickly. She is smashing props, ripping costumes to shreds. Accusing me, me Andre de Croissant of planning an infidelity. *(To himself.)* Who knew she could hear from that far off stage? *Back to PRATT.)* Please I beg of you. You see before you a desperate desperate man.

PRATT. Well actually I just got this piece in. It is a steal at only sixty thousand francs. I would think the lady would be thrilled to own something this unique.

ANDRE. *(Quickly counting out money, grabbing the trinket and turning to go.)* Thank you Madame, you have saved my life.

PRATT. *(Trying to stop him.)* But sir … there is something …sir. … Well, I guess he will learn soon enough of the engraving inside … of the name … Evangeline.

(BLACKOUT; Spot up on EVANGELINE.)

EVANGELINE. *(Aside to audience as she walks out of the shadows.)* Is it possible I could be so blind? Is Miss Pratt right? Could it be what I have been looking for was right under my nose the whole time?

MUSIC: AT LONG LAST LOVE

EVANGELINE.
I'M SO IN LOVE
AND THOUGH IT GIVES ME JOY INTENSE
I CAN'T DECIPHER
IF I'M A LIFER,
OR IF IT'S JUST A FIRST OFFENSE
I'M SO IN LOVE,
I'VE NO SENSE OF VALUES LEFT AT ALL.
IS THIS A PLAYTIME,
AFFAIR OF MAYTIME
OR IS IT A WINDFALL?

IS IT AN EARTHQUAKE OR SIMPLY A SHOCK?
IS IT THE GOOD TURTLE SOUP OR MERELY THE MOCK?
IS IT A COCKTAIL-THIS FEELING OF JOY,
OR IS WHAT I FEEL THE REAL MCCOY?

HAVE I THE RIGHT HUNCH OR HAVE I THE WRONG?
WILL IT BE BACH I SHALL HEAR OR JUST A COLE PORTER
    SONG?
IS IT A FANCY NOT WORTH THINKING OF,
OR IS IT AT LONG LAST LOVE?

IS IT THE RAINBOW OR JUST A MIRAGE?
WILL IT BE TENDER AND SWEET OR MERELY MASSAGE?
WHAT CAN ACCOUNT FOR THESE STRANGE PITTER-
    PATS?
COULD THIS BE THE DREAM, THE CREAM, THE CAT'S?
IS IT FOR ALL TIME OR SIMPLY A LARK?
IS IT A BOLT FROM THE BLUE OR JUST A LEAP IN THE
    DARK?
SHOULD I SAY "THUMBS DOWN" AND GIVE IT A SHOVE,
OR IS IT AT LONG LAST LOVE?

IS IT TO RESCUE OR IS IT TO WRECK?
IS IT AN ACHE IN THE HEART OR JUST A PAIN IN THE
    NECK?

IS IT THE IVY YOU TOUCH WITH A GLOVE,
OR IS IT AT LONG LAST LOVE?

(BLACKOUT.)

End of Scene 3

Scene 4

Scene: A garden in Oxford, England.
Time: Several days later.
At Rise: Trees and flowers come in; a wishing well moves forward; a
table with umbrella and chairs enter until all resembles a
typical English garden. Evangeline's AUNT ERMYNTRUDE,
an elderly, senile woman, sits in one of the chairs. On the
table before her are a watering can, a teapot and a teacup.

AUNTIE. You know, when these irises reach full bloom, they
will be stunning. *(Tilting her head as if listening to someone.)* I was
thinking we should get arbors for the climbers to train on. *(She picks
up the teapot to pour herself a cup, but is distracted.)* Is it just me, or
do those daisies look in dire straits? *(Still holding the teapot, she rises
and crosses to the bed of daisies.)* Are you thirsty little ones?
(Dousing them with steaming hot tea.) There you are. *(She absent-
mindedly sets the tea pot down next to the flowers and strolls about.
Suddenly she starts swatting at the air.)* No, no. Go away. Back to
your hive. Back I say. *(Following the bee's flight as it moves away.)* I
think it thought me a daffodil and was trying to pollinate me. *(She
chuckles to herself and returns to the table, where she pours water
from the watering can into her teacup and takes a sip.)* Perhaps I
should have let it steep a bit longer.

*(EVANGELINE, now in a suitable travel outfit, enters carrying a pas-
try box.)*

EVANGELINE. Hello, Auntie.
AUNTIE. Why Evangeline. *(Looking at her watch.)* You're late
my dear.
EVANGELINE. *(Holding out the box.)* I stopped to pick up your
favorite pastries.
AUNTIE. Oh well, no wonder then. How lovely.
EVANGELINE. I'm glad to be home at last. The gardens look

wonderful.

AUNTIE. Yes, it has been a good year for them. A great deal of growth. *(Looking closely at EVANGELINE)* You look pale my dear. Are you all right?

EVANGELINE. I'm just a little tired. It has been a long journey.

AUNTIE. *(Picking up the watering can.)* I'll make another pot of tea. This one seems a trifle weak.

(She exits with the watering can. EVANGELINE drops into a chair. There is humming and the sound of hedge clippers; she looks around.)

EVANGELINE. What the devil? *(Suddenly, VICTOR pops up from behind a bush; he continues to clip away. Aside to audience.)* Maybe there is something to this fate thing. *(Calling out.)* Victor!

(Turning and seeing her, he accidentally clips a big chunk from a bush.)

VICTOR. Look what you made me do. I've been trying to forget you. So, why on earth are you here?

EVANGELINE. This property belongs to my aunt. Your excuse would be?

VICTOR. I was hired to develop the grounds and gardens. But now, knowing of your presence, I shall respect your wishes and leave immediately.

EVANGELINE. Victor, wait. Maybe I wish for you to stay.

VICTOR. Why? Why this sudden change?

EVANGELINE. Oh, I was a perfect idiot with you. I left school thinking I was so worldly-wise, and knew all the answers. Victor, I have been thinking. About a lot of things. Love. Fate. Us.

VICTOR. There is no us. You made that very clear in Paris. And, for that matter, every time I saw you.

EVANGELINE. A lady is entitled to change her mind. And her heart.

VICTOR. Yes, but a gentleman doesn't have to wait until she does. Good-bye.

EVANGELINE. I'm sure you will find someplace else to garden.

VICTOR. Garden? My profession is horticulture. It is much more than gardening. It is the science of cultivating plants and flowers.

(He turns to exit; EVANGELINE crosses, trying to think of something to say.)

EVANGELINE. Is that so? Then, as a man of science can you honestly say— Do you think you have truthfully and fully explored and exhausted all the possibilities? Well, do you?

VICTOR. *(Stopping and turning toward her.)* Possibilities. The possibilities of what?

EVANGELINE. Of, of *cultivating* this relationship. You and me. *(Imploring.)* Couldn't you give it ~~just one more~~ chance?

VICTOR. *(Softening up.)* I don't know. ~~I don't want to be hurt again.~~

MUSIC: EXPERIMENT / FINALE

EVANGELINE.
AS I WAS LEAVING HIGH SCHOOL
MY PET PROFESSOR OF MY SCHOOL
SAID: MY DEAR, ONE PARTING MESSAGE I WOULD GIVE
    TO YOU.
DO WHAT ALL GOOD SCIENTISTS DO.
EXPERIMENT
WHENEVER DOUBTFUL TAKE A CHANCE
EXPERIMENT
AND YOU'LL DISCOVER SWEET ROMANCE
WHEN IN A STATE OF IGNORANT BLISS
REGARDING A CREATURE YOU CRAVE
'TIS FOLLY, MY FRIEND, TO BEHAVE.

EXPERIMENT
BE CURIOUS.
AND WHEN YOU'VE PICKED A PERFECT WIFE.
GET FURIOUS
TILL SHE IS YOURS AND YOURS FOR LIFE.
IF THIS YOU DO (AND NO COCK-AND-BULL)
IN TIME SHE MAY GIVE YOU A NURS'RY FULL
OF MERRIMENT.

VICTOR. *(Coming around.)* Is that a promise?
EVANGELINE. Experiment. And you'll see.

(By the end of this section, she has won VICTOR over; they joyfully embrace and then exit arm in arm. There is a dramatic change in the lighting; everything becomes even brighter, like a golden summer day. Suddenly, a bunch of flowers begins to rise. It turns out to be the flowered hat of MISS PRATT, who appears in a bridesmaid dress.)

PRATT.
AND NOW, EACH ONE OF YOU, DO
LET ME ADAPT THIS DITTY TO YOU.
EXPERIMENT
MAKE IT YOUR MOTTO DAY AND NIGHT.
EXPERIMENT
AND IT WILL LEAD YOU TO THE LIGHT.
THE APPLE ON THE TOP OF THE TREE
IS NEVER TOO HIGH TO ACHIEVE,
SO TAKE AN EXAMPLE FROM EVE,
EXPERIMENT

(Other bunches of flowers begin to rise in the garden. They are the
hats of JOYCE, HENRIETTA, BERTHA and MADELINE, who
are also dressed as bridesmaids.)

GIRLS.
BE CURIOUS
THOUGH INTERFERING FRIENDS MAY FROWN,
GET FURIOUS
AT EACH ATTEMPT TO HOLD YOU DOWN.
IF THIS ADVICE YOU ONLY EMPLOY
THE FUTURE CAN OFFER YOU INFINITE JOY
AND MERRIMENT.
EXPERIMENT
AND YOU'LL SEE.

(EVANGELINE and VICTOR return dressed as bride and groom;
they take center stage as the entire company joins in the ener-
gized finale.)

ALL.
EXPERIMENT
MAKE IT YOUR MOTTO DAY AND NIGHT.
EXPERIMENT
AND IT WILL LEAD YOU TO THE LIGHT.
THE APPLE ON THE TOP OF THE TREE
IS NEVER TOO HIGH TO ACHIEVE,
SO TAKE AN EXAMPLE FROM EVE,
EXPERIMENT
BE CURIOUS
THOUGH INTERFERING FRIENDS MAY FROWN,
GET FURIOUS
AT EACH ATTEMPT TO HOLD YOU DOWN.
IF THIS ADVICE YOU ONLY EMPLOY

THE FUTURE CAN OFFER YOU INFINITE JOY
AND MERRIMENT.
EXPERIMENT
AND YOU'LL SEE.
THAT'S WHAT FOLKS SAY
EXPERIMENT.

*(On the last line, EVANGELINE throws her wedding bouquet to the
orchestra conductor, who catches it and gives a sheepish look out
to the audience.)*

CURTAIN